Always Faithful

Young Single Austens

WS Deming

Little Gray House

First edition 2020

Dedication

To Dad, Master Gunnery-Sergeant Douglas Deming, Sr., Ret.
and all the military people in my family
Thank you for your service.

CONTENTS

Chapter 1

"I will miss you guys so much!" Paige yelled as her classroom emptied on the last of day school. "Be good over the summer!"

"Miss Ellis, Miss Ellis!" A little boy with dark brown hair collided into her. He wrapped his little arms around her waist. She hugged him back.

"Why can't you be my teacher next year?" he said, giving her big puppy dog eyes.

"Because I teach third grade. You're growing up and moving on to fourth grade with Mrs. White and Mrs. Austen," Paige said. "You'll love them. They are so much fun."

A harried-looking woman rushed into the room.

"Caleb!" she said. "I'm so sorry, Miss Ellis. I've got the baby out in the car. Come on, Caleb, we need to go."

"I'm glad you were in my class this year, buddy," Paige said. "Remember what I told you about my soldier friend? His name was Caleb, too."

"He's always helping people," little Caleb said.

"That's right."

"Did he get to fire a gun?"

"Probably," she said, smiling. "Your mom and baby sister need you this summer to be like big Caleb and help out, okay?"

"Okay," he said, though he didn't look enthusiastic. "But soldiers don't have to take care of babies."

"You have a great summer, and I'll see you in the halls next year!"

Little Caleb hugged her one more time and then grabbed his mother by the hand.

"Thanks, Miss Ellis," Caleb's mom said. "You have a wonderful summer."

"Thanks, you too," Paige said.

As soon as the door shut, she leaned against her desk. Wonderful, an entire summer of doing nothing but prepping for next year; she grimaced.

She picked up her phone. There was a text from Elliot.

Dinner at 7 tonight?

Sure, meet you at the restaurant. Send me the address.

Will do. See you then.

She sighed. Elliot was a nice enough guy. Nice enough she'd given him a couple of chances to take her out. There was no spark for her there, but he seemed to enjoy her company. Going out with him was better than sitting in her pajamas on a Friday night, watching *Supernatural* reruns.

She perused the rest of her texts. There was one from her sister, Lindsay, asking Paige to watch her kids on Saturday. There was one from her mom, asking if she wanted to spend the first week of summer vacation at home with them. Then there was a text from Alisa, her best friend and big Caleb's twin sister. Big Caleb really was a soldier in the Marines somewhere in South Carolina, though he flew jets more than he fired guns these days.

Thinking of Caleb, even after all these years, still brought up a bag of mixed emotions for Paige—hurt, regret, sadness, and longing. Alisa, as much as she loved her brother, understood Paige's feelings and sympathized. The two friends had an unspoken understanding between them—Caleb was like "Fight Club"—you don't ask about Caleb, and you don't talk about Caleb. Or rather, Alisa stayed away from topics that involved Caleb directly, and Paige never asked Alisa direct questions about him.

You need to call me as soon as school gets out.

Paige raised an eyebrow. Alisa wasn't usually this mysterious. Paige's cute, straight-forward best friend usually just said what was on her mind. Her down-to-earth personality was the perfect yin to Paige's passionate and fun-loving yang. Paige missed Alisa sometimes. Alisa felt compelled to be with her twin as he moved from base to base during his career as a soldier. The twins were extraordinarily close, and nothing made Alisa happier than taking care of someone. Paige was sure Caleb had no objection whatsoever to having his sister spoil him rotten.

Paige dialed her friend's phone number. Alisa picked it up on the second ring.

"Hey!" Alisa said. "How are you doing?"

"Um, fine," Paige said. "How's South Carolina?"

"Sunny. And warm, and I'm so excited, Paige!"

"Okay," Paige said, now starting to feel excited for her best friend.

"So you remember Tom, right?" Alisa asked, giggling.

Both Paige's eyebrows shot up. Alisa didn't giggle much.

"Yes, the helicopter pilot in the Marines? The one with the gorgeous green eyes? The one you've been dating for a while?"

Alisa actually sighed. "Yes. That one."

"Yes," Paige said, a smile spreading across her face.

"Well, he asked me to marry him last night—and I said yes!" Alisa practically squealed.

"Shut the front door!" Paige said. A text message notification sounded from her phone.

"Check that message I sent you."

Paige opened her messages, and there, sparkling back at her, was a huge diamond solitaire hanging off Alisa's hand.

"Oh my goodness, it is so beautiful! How did he propose?"

"He took me out to Hilton Head. We went walking on the beach near sunset. The next thing I know, he's kneeling on the sand in front of me. He said he loved me from the first moment he saw me and wants to spend the rest of his life with me."

"Oh, how romantic!" Paige said. "I am so excited for you, Alisa. Everything you've told me about him makes me like him so much. You guys will be so happy."

"Thank you. I think so too. And I need to ask you something else."

"Oh?"

"Would you be my maid of honor?"

"Oh, Lise, I would love to!"

"Well, I couldn't have anyone else. You are my best friend."

"When are you getting married?"

"July 10, 2015."

"Say what now?" Paige asked. "You mean like this July 10th?"

"Yes. Training for both Caleb and Tom is in August. If we want time to get married and go on a small honeymoon, it's got to be quick. They both had a ton of leave saved up, so they'll be taking three weeks off. Even so, it's got to be in July because of the training."

"Oh, that's not much time to get something put together," Paige said.

"You know my mom. It'll be planned before I even get there," she said. "I just need to schedule a temple sealing date and time, and pick out a dress."

"Okay, which temple?"

"The Salt Lake Temple."

"You're coming here?" Paige said. "I'm so thrilled you're coming here! I can't wait to see you!"

"We need to spend as much time together as we can when I'm there," Alisa said. "I promise Caleb will be on his best behavior."

Paige's breath caught in her throat for a moment. She would see Caleb again after all these years. Guilt and trepidation replaced the initial thrill.

"I'm not worried about him," Paige said, trying her hardest to sound unimpressed. "I can't wait to see you and meet Tom. This will be so much fun. I have all summer to help you out!"

"I knew you'd be so excited for me," Alisa said. She sighed. "Mom and Dad were excited when I told them Tom and I were getting married. They got upset when I told them we were getting sealed in the temple. My dad wanted the whole big church wedding with walking me down the aisle and everything. Now they say Tom ruined it all."

"Oh, Lise, I'm sorry," Paige said. "Lots of people do ring ceremonies. The reception center can set up an aisle he can walk you down, and you and Tom can exchange rings."

"I already told my dad that," she said. "He doesn't care. He says it's not the same."

"Maybe he'll get more into the spirit the closer to the date we get."

"I doubt that," Alisa said. "He's still pissed Caleb and I joined the Church. He thought for sure we'd escaped the Church's clutches when we moved to Florida for Caleb's flight training."

"Just pray for them," Paige said. "Even if they never accept the fact you joined the Church, they should still find it in them to love their new son-in-law and support their only daughter."

“You’re probably right,” Alisa said. “All that aside though, I’m so excited to see you and introduce you to Tom.”

“Me too,” Paige said.

CHAPTER 2

Paige parked her car and rushed into the restaurant. Scanning the dining area, she found Elliot sitting at a table by himself. Paige grimaced. Late, as always. She wondered why he put up with it. He looked content enough and smiled at her when he finally saw her walking toward the table.

"I am so sorry I'm late again," Paige said.

"It's fine," he said, pulling her chair out for her. They opened the menus, and she glanced at him. Most women would consider him cute. His blond, curly hair, slim build, and pleasant smile attracted the attention of quite a few of the women in the ward, but he'd chosen Paige. It wasn't everyday she found a guy who could converse intelligently, who listened instead of talking all the time, and liked her as a person. But cordial friendliness was the most she had mustered for him. Elliot liked her a lot more than she did him, and she hadn't been able to feel more for the lawyer.

The server took their order. Paige waited for Elliot to say something, but he seemed content to sit and enjoy the ambiance of the restaurant. She sighed. She was going to have to get something started if she didn't want to have to sit in silence until dinner came.

"We're celebrating today," she said, trying to ease the slight awkwardness.

"We are?" he asked.

"Yes. It's the last day of the school year. I'm free as a bird until mid-August."

"That's definitely a benefit to being a schoolteacher. You get summers off."

"Not this year, though. I found out today my best friend is getting married in July, and she asked me to be her maid of honor."

"Congratulations," he said. "That will keep you busy."

"Definitely, and I've got all summer to help her out."

"So that's your only plan for the summer?"

"So far. Um, how's everything going at your firm?"

"Good," he said. "Lots of paperwork. Lots of filing. Um, my firm is having a company party at the end of June. I'd ask you to come, but it sounds like you will be busy."

"Yeah, I would hate to commit to something and then have to bow out at the last minute."

He nodded. "The invitation's open if things slow down at all."

They ate their food in silence when it came. Conversation flowed better when one person picked up the slack if the other person didn't know what else to say. Caleb never had a problem with that. If there wasn't anything specific to talk about, he'd bring up any random old thing, and they'd be laughing hysterically before too long.

Since the evening appeared pleasant, they walked around downtown afterward.

"Could I ask you a question?"

"Sure."

"At the risk of sounding insecure, do you genuinely like me, or are you going out with me merely because I ask?"

The question caught her off guard. It was not a topic of conversation she'd expected to have right at that moment. She wasn't sure how she would answer without being a heel.

"I'm sorry," he said, shaking his head. "I guess a question like that is a little unfair. It's the lawyer in me. I shouldn't have sprung it on you like that."

"It was unexpected," she said, smiling at him, trying to make up for her lack of response. "I do genuinely like you, Elliot. Beyond that, I'm not sure I could give you a fair answer."

"Thank you for being honest with me," he said. "I like you too. I'm trying to figure you out, Paige. I'm glad you like me. I would like to think we have a good time together."

"I don't believe in leading on perfectly affable men," Paige said. "I would let you know if I felt it wasn't worth your time, or mine."

"Okay, good," he said, smiling at her.

"I'm glad you said something. It will be so crazy these next few weeks with the wedding. I might not have a lot of extra time. I didn't want it to come across as me trying to avoid you."

"I understand."

They reached Temple Square. Deep purples and blues blanketed the skies above them, highlighting the brightly lit temple. They sat down together at the reflection pool in the plaza and looked up at the grand granite building.

"I always had this plan in my head," Elliot said. "I'd return from my mission and 'the one' would wait for me to come home to find her. We'd have a whirlwind romance and get married here for time and all eternity. It's funny how life doesn't work out the way we planned."

"I know what you mean," Paige said. "Once upon a time, I almost married someone. It would have been a civil ceremony because he wasn't a member. I didn't settle because I believe temple marriage is important. Besides, marriage is hard enough without being unevenly yoked and all that."

"I'm sure you are glad you didn't settle," he said. "Temple marriage is important. I think that's why I've been single for so long. If you make that kind of commitment to someone, you need to be sure you're with the right person."

"Exactly. I made the right decision, as hard as it was at the time. The only part I regret is, it didn't end well because he didn't understand the reasons for it."

"Whatever happened to that long-lost love of yours?"

"The last I heard, he flew jets for the Marines in South Carolina."

"I'd say if you loved someone enough, you'd do whatever it takes to be together."

"It's more complicated than that. Flirt to convert may work for some, but I would always wonder. Did he join the Church to make me happy, or because he really believed in it?"

"Point taken. Being a new convert is hard enough without having a strong testimony as the foundation."

Paige smiled at him. He impressed her for once. She sensed he really understood her for the first time. She enjoyed being able to talk to someone about her past with Caleb. Talking about it helped ease the nervousness that had been building since Alisa called earlier in the day, even if she was being fairly vague.

Curiosity warred with apprehension when she thought of Caleb. They'd be seeing a lot of each other in the next few weeks. Paige worried his resentment toward her was still as strong as it had been ten years ago. She hoped not. Still, a disappointment that profound wasn't something anyone forgot about either.

She hated reminding herself of the worst night of her life. Caleb had walked away so angry, nothing she could do or say would help him understand better. Paige was even more devastated when Alisa told her Caleb had already left for and completed boot camp before she was even aware he'd left. She missed out on the chance to explain things better when emotions weren't so high. He assumed she was telling him he wasn't good enough for her. She never got to tell him how wrong he had been.

Her parents offered paltry comfort. Even though their objections to the marriage went beyond the religious difference, they felt strongly Paige had made the right decision. Wally and Liz both knew how military life worked. Wally had been in the army; Liz had been an army wife for over ten years. What would Paige do, they said, when almost as soon as they got married Caleb would be off to boot camp? He'd be leaving Paige alone in a strange city for more than a year while he also finished his training school. What would she do with Caleb gone all the time on multiple deployments? What if they had kids? How would she finish school as a single parent? Would she even be able to finish school?

Those were just the secular concerns. Without a temple sealing, Paige risked losing Caleb every time he deployed to a war zone. Would he be unsupportive of her activity in the Church? Or would she fall away because it was easier to be with him and how he lived rather than being active? Or would any children they had together decide Dad's way was better than Mom's? They weren't wrong, not even a little.

That hadn't made watching him walk away through her tears any easier. The absolute devastation on Caleb's face after Paige rejected him still cracked her heart, even after all these years. Principles didn't comfort her when the one person she loved best in the world walked out of her life. It didn't soothe the jagged pieces of her heart, knowing he felt the same way about her. She'd never been able to shake the sense she'd made a horrible mistake that day.

Truth be told, Elliot stood little chance at capturing Paige's heart, and he hadn't been the first. She compared every man she dated with Caleb. Nothing compared to the effortless way she and Caleb had been together. With Caleb, they fit together seamlessly where a deep connection, felicity, humor, and easy rapport was there from the beginning. She first noticed it when he'd approached her at that dance in high school their junior year. Even though she was nervous, he soon had her giggling and relaxed with his open and silly conversation. From that moment on, they sought each other out every day. They declared nothing officially—they were together from then on. Sometimes, Paige feared she idealized their relationship, focusing on all the positive stuff but forgetting anything bad. But despite it being a hard standard to live up to, only a stronger, more exceptional connection would have tempted Paige to replace Caleb in her heart.

Later that night, Paige looked through her junior and senior year yearbooks. She examined Caleb's face. He'd been a tall, but not gawky kid, with a sweet smile and teasing sense of fun. He looked slightly different now. She'd never admit it, but she social-media stalked him occasionally, just to see how he was doing. Alisa was her best friend, so it wasn't hard. He looked like he'd grown wider, his face more masculine.

She looked at that boyish, high school face of his and wondered why he'd never gotten married either. Alisa went on for days about military groupies who flocked to the different bases and ports, trying to land themselves a military husband. Caleb, thankfully, didn't seem interested in any of that. So, it wasn't for lack of effort from the female population of the United States that he remained single. She worried their break-up had damaged his ability to see relationships as overall good things, but then that would give *her* too much credit. Maybe it had made him more picky. She was glad he was still single. It was selfish of her, she knew. The notion of him belonging to someone else made her feel a little sick, but she also didn't want him to be lonely. Alisa's marriage to Tom would change the dynamic between Caleb and his sister. They were all on the younger side of thirty, and with Alisa getting married, he'd consider settling down himself. Regardless, one thing she was sure of—her chance with Caleb was over. He'd been too angry and hurt the last time they saw each other. He wouldn't have recovered from something so painful.

CHAPTER 3

Paige paced back and forth in the open entrance to Salt Lake International Airport. She'd promised Alisa she'd pick up the three of them coming in from South Carolina from the airport. It had been so long since they'd seen each other, and the days were about to be so crazy. If Paige picked them up, Alisa and Paige would have a few extra minutes to chat before they got to Bountiful. She'd get to meet Tom in person. The only problem with the plan is she'd have to see Caleb, too.

Paige's anxiety spiked as she looked at the arrivals board. No sign of them, even though the once-delayed flight had arrived. She was excited to see her best friend again. She couldn't wait to meet Tom. She dreaded seeing Caleb.

From across the room near the baggage claim, she heard her name ringing across the distance. "Paige!"

Paige turned, and there was Alisa running toward her. She pulled her friend into a fierce hug. "Lise! I'm so glad you guys finally made it."

"Oh, it's so good to see you again," Alisa said after pulling away. "You look amazing. I mean, you're different in such a good way."

"Thank you," Paige said. "You're glowing. Seriously, not kidding. You are."

Alisa turned around. A pair of young men came up to them, toting luggage. She recognized Tom from his pictures on Alisa's social media. The other was Caleb.

Paige tried everything in her power to maintain her composure, but she realized after a minute she'd stopped breathing. Being in the Marines had done Caleb a world of good. She knew he'd be different, but she didn't appreciate how much until he stood in front of her. He'd added muscle to the height of him, and his face was no longer boyish. He still had the same smirky grin, but he was a full-grown man now. She tore her eyes away from him when Alisa grabbed her hand.

"Tom, this is my very best friend, Paige Ellis," she said.

"It's nice to meet you finally," Tom replied, giving her a firm handshake. He had the most remarkable green eyes and a clean smile. "Lise talks about you so much it's like we're already acquainted."

"I know! I'm excited to meet you in person," Paige said. "I couldn't be happier for you both."

She finally allowed herself to look over at Caleb again. "Hello, Caleb. How are you?"

"I'm fine, Paige. Good to see you again," he said. There was very little inflection in his voice and no warmth at all. It was as she suspected. He was still angry. She sighed inwardly.

"Well, let's get you packed up and headed off to Bountiful," Paige said, as she led them out of the terminal. "My car is just across the way in the parking lot."

"Can we stop somewhere to get a bite to eat? I'm starved," Alisa said as they were putting the luggage in the trunk.

"Sure. What are you in the mood for?"

"Big, tall, disgustingly high-calorie shakes."

"All you had to do is ask," Paige replied, giving her best friend a wide grin.

Tom held the passenger side door open for Alisa when they got to Paige's car. "Here, babe, sit in front so you and Paige can talk. Us POGs will sit back and enjoy the ride."

"Thanks," Alisa said before giving Tom a sweet kiss.

"What in the world is a POG?" Paige asked Tom.

"Personnel Other than Grunts," Tom said.

Paige laughed. "That is so weird. I love it."

Alisa looked over at Paige with an enormous smile on her face. The smile lit up her face so much it glowed. Paige's heart burst with happiness. She'd never seen Alisa this happy—ever. And Tom was so sweet and gentlemanly. Alisa had definitely caught an excellent one.

They drove down the freeway, and when they got closer to downtown Salt Lake, Alisa gushed. "It's so different."

"It's not that different," Paige said.

"No, seriously, there are a ton of new buildings. Tom, over there you can see the temple. I'm so excited, Paige. I'm getting married in a fairy-tale castle."

"So, Paige, Lise tells me you teach elementary school," Tom said.

"Yes, third grade," she answered. "I love it. The kids are a handful, but they are adorable and so loving. They want to learn and to please their teacher, most of the time."

"That's great," Tom said. "Lise said you've always loved kids."

"That's true," Paige said, smiling at Tom in the rearview mirror. She looked over at Caleb. He had a thoughtful expression on his face as he looked back at her. "I love other people's, but I can't wait to have my own."

"It'll happen," Tom stated. "I didn't think I'd have to wait until I was twenty-seven to find the one, but it was worth the wait."

Moisture pooled in Paige's eyes and, when she looked over at her, Alisa had the same. What a sweet thing to say. She hoped when she finally found the right one, he'd say things like that, too.

"Tom, knock off being so sweet," Caleb said. "You're making the ladyfolk tear up."

Tom reached over the seat and squeezed Alisa's shoulder.

"It's how I feel about you," Tom said.

"So, Tom, um, you and Caleb are both pilots, right?" Paige asked.

"Yes, I fly helicopters, and he flies jets," he said. "Best job in the world. It's how we became friends. We'd run into each other all the time on base."

"I'm glad you met them. You've been a blessing in more ways than one," Paige said, trying her hardest to avoid Caleb's gaze. "When we were younger, religion wasn't a topic that came up very often. I mean, it was always around us, because Alisa and Caleb spent a lot of time at my house. My parents were sticklers for Alisa and Caleb to follow *For the Strength of Youth* standards while they were at my house, but it's not like my parents sat around and held discussions about what the Church believes with them. They weren't ready for that message yet. I did a terrible job at explaining it."

Paige cleared her throat and kept her focus on the road. "I was so excited and thankful to find out they'd been investigating and baptized into our church because of you. The timing has to be right, I guess."

"That's been my experience too," Tom said. "When I was on my mission in France, I'd meet people who seemed to have been searching for something. They didn't know what, and it seemed to take their entire lives, but they could never find it. And then you'd met people who'd never given it a moment's thought until you talked to them. Then their entire world changes."

"Well, if nothing else, I thank you very much," Paige said. "Alisa and I have been best friends since first meeting each other. Now the gospel is one more thing we share that I will be forever grateful for. Not to mention I'm sure we're both grateful that you and Caleb have the Spirit to guide you when you're deployed."

"It's kind of interesting. When you're flying aircraft or you're overseas somewhere, you rely on the Lord a lot. The only thing I can compare it to is being on a mission. It's then you really understand how very mindful He is of you personally."

"I completely agree," Paige said. "I think I'd never been as close to the Lord or had as strong a testimony as when I was on my mission."

"You went on a mission? Where to?" Tom asked.

"Australia Darwin Mission."

"That's cool," Tom said.

"You went on a mission?" Caleb said.

"I did. I've been back about six years now. Lise, you didn't tell him I was in Australia?"

"I thought I did," Alisa said. "But he's been busy being a Marine and a pilot and didn't join the Church until a few years ago, so why would I have?"

"Okay," Caleb said, shrugging. "Cool."

Paige nodded, but tried not to roll her eyes. *Well, gee, Caleb, it's nice to know you really don't care.*

She could see Tom looking back and forth between the two, but he said nothing.

"So, Lise, do you have a plan for the next few weeks?"

"Yes. Well, my mom does. I'm pretty sure we'll barely have to do a thing. Mom said she's got a lot of appointments set up already, so we'll just go one step at a time. I hope you don't mind that it will be one appointment after the other."

"Honey, you have me at your beck and call for the entire summer. I'm planning on enjoying every second," Paige said, smiling as she pulled up to the restaurant.

Tom jumped out of the backseat and opened the door for Alisa before she could.

"Seems someone's momma raised them right," Paige said, laughing.

"Yes, ma'am," Tom said, taking Alisa's hand to help her out of the car.

Alisa took a big, dramatic breath in. "Burgers," Alisa said, happily sighing.

Caleb jetted for the door of the restaurant to open it for everyone. As Paige passed by Caleb, she got a little dizzy. The height and bulk he'd attained in the Marines only added to his looming presence. He had a heavenly smelling cologne. All of that combined was overwhelming.

"I'm paying," Tom said.

"No, you're not," Caleb said.

"Yes, I got this."

"Seriously, let me get it this time."

Alisa and Paige looked at each other, amused.

"You're here to marry my sister, not pick up the tab for everything," Caleb said. He approached the ordering counter and blocked the cash machine with his body.

"Really, you guys?" Alisa said. "You don't have to do this to impress Paige."

"I'm not," Caleb said, staring icily at Paige. Turning away, he tried to lighten the mood. "If I let this joker pay all the time, you'll have to step up your graphic design game to pay for it."

Caleb's face was like a punch to the gut. She understood he might resent her still, but did he have to be such a jerk about it? Paige's appetite disappeared. She folded her arms across her chest and wandered over to the seating area. She found a table where all of them would fit and pulled out her phone. Paige's mother and Lindsay had blown up her phone asking if Alisa had arrived yet. She answered them until the others joined her.

Alisa sat next to Paige and rubbed her arm. "You forgot to order," Alisa said. "So, I got you a small peanut-butter-cup shake. I hope that's okay."

"Yes, thank you, Lise," Paige said, not allowing herself to glance at Caleb. She might sprout tears if she did. His icy countenance was more disturbing than knowing the reason for it. There was a small part of her that hoped they could be on friendly terms before the wedding was over. Seemed Caleb had no such plan.

The three from South Carolina chatted about life at the military base until an employee brought their food. Paige played with her shake. It effectively shut Paige out of the conversation. Not that she minded. She didn't feel like talking, and the gossip of the military branch and life in Beaufort was entertaining.

"So, Paige," Tom said. "Where do you teach?"

"It's called Ascent Academy. It's in West Jordan, which is south of here. I have a nice apartment that's not too far from there, as well."

"Is Ascent Academy a private school?"

"No, it's a charter school. It's independent of the state school district, but it's still a public school. I like the freedom to teach in a way I think will benefit each of my students."

"I notice you found a profession where you're always the smartest person in the room," Caleb said. "What's it like to always have the upper hand?"

"Caleb!" Alisa exclaimed.

"I don't know about always having the upper hand. There are days when my TA and I wonder what Kool-Aid all the kids drank that morning," Paige said, facing Caleb. "What about you? Seems you found a job where your head is always in the clouds."

Caleb chuckled. "Still clever with words, as usual." The dimple in his cheek when he laughed was still there, and Paige's stomach did a few flips.

"How do you do it?" Tom said. "All those kids all day long."

"I could say the same about you two," Paige said. "How can you constantly fly with nothing between you and the ground but air? I hate flying in a commercial plane, let alone something only designed to carry one or two."

"It's the rush," Tom said. "That feeling of all that horsepower under your control."

"You, too?" Paige said smiling. "I knew Caleb was an adrenaline junkie, so I suppose it shouldn't surprise me you are, too."

"You're an adrenaline junkie that should play it safer these days," Caleb said, elbowing Tom in the ribs. "I'm not going to let you leave my sister a widow, if I can help it."

"Psh, just because you're stubbornly single doesn't mean you can be as careless as you want, little brother," Alisa said.

"Little brother by five minutes," Caleb said, giving his sister the most genuine smile Paige had seen since meeting again at the airport. That was at least one thing he hadn't grown out of since high school. His smile was still as cheeky and brilliant as she remembered it.

"Well, it's nearly two o'clock," Caleb said, looking at his watch. "I think it's time to face the music."

"Good luck," Paige said. "Once I drop you off, call me if there's anything else I can do to help. I'll be over at my parents' house."

"You might regret making that offer," Alisa said, looking markedly more nervous than she had been a few minutes ago. She clung to Tom's hand.

"I'll just stay at my parents' house until the wedding," Paige said. "My mom already invited me to stay for the beginning of summer. Then I won't have to travel to Bountiful from West Jordan every time we need to go do something."

Paige pulled up to the Watsons' house a short while later, stared at the brown brick rambler, and sighed. Even though she still came to visit her parents and sister with relative frequency, when she came to Bountiful, she avoided this street. She still had wonderful memories of coming to this house. Karen and Ted had welcomed Paige at first. They were grateful their daughter had met a nice friend so quickly after moving to a new area in the middle of her junior year. Things changed when Paige and Caleb became more than friends. Karen tolerated the romance mostly because Paige was a good girl. But Paige frequently found herself answering questions about Mormonism. After each session, Karen seemed to be less and less satisfied with Paige's presence around the house. Karen and Ted were never outrightly hostile to Paige, but their warmth had long disappeared before the end of the friends' senior year.

Paige watched Caleb as everyone got their luggage out of the car. His focus was elsewhere, and she had an uninterrupted view of him. Definitely more handsome than in high school. He moved with strength and grace. Through Alisa, she knew Caleb had worked hard for all he'd earned in the Marines. He'd started out enlisted, but then got through school as quickly as his duties would let him and earned his commission. That's when his dreams of flying planes really took off, so to speak. He flew fighter jets, and there wasn't a more perfect occupation for him. She'd always known him to be a risk taker and completely unafraid of new experiences. These qualities attracted her to him from the first. She wasn't good at taking risks—she overthought everything. But when she had been with him during high school, anything seemed possible. His grit and his ambition definitely increased his appeal. But then he'd opened his mouth at the restaurant. It was tempting to hug and smack him at the same time. His icy look and his rude exclamation about her still smarted.

Caleb didn't look at her. She didn't really expect him to. If he still resented her from all those years ago, she definitely deserved some of it. Maybe now that he was a member, she could properly explain to him all the things she'd wished to say the night she'd turned down his marriage proposal. She could hope he'd finally understand her side of the story, and apologize to him like she'd wanted to for a long time. It was probably too much to expect his forgiveness. She vowed before he left for South Carolina, she'd take a chance to talk to him alone.

CHAPTER 4

Paige knocked on the door of her sister, Lindsay's, cute two-story. It was in one of the newly built neighborhoods of Bountiful, not too far from their parents' house. Screams erupted from behind the door and a very frazzled-looking Lindsay answered. Baby Will sat on her hip pulling her hair, and Cameron came flying through the doorway into Paige's arms.

"Paige!" the little boy yelled.

"Why are you screaming?" Paige asked him as she walked into the door.

"I am a dinosaur," he said, making claws with his hands, letting out another ear-piercing scream instead of a roar.

"Oh, boy, you scared me to death," Paige said.

"Brent isn't here yet. He got stuck at work. Let's go into the TV room," Lindsay said.

Paige put Dinosaur Cameron down and took Will from his mother. "Where's my smile?" she said, tickling the baby. "Are you going to give your Auntie Paige a smile?"

The baby's face erupted into a smile, showing off his two bottom teeth. "There they are. There are those cute little teeth." Paige looked at her sister. "Are the top ones coming in yet?"

"Yes," Lindsay said. "He's trying to chew on everything, including me."

"Aww, are you trying to eat your momma?" Paige said, squeezing his chubby cheeks. He giggled and grabbed her hand. It promptly went in his mouth, and he started gnawing on her fingers. "Ow, hey there. Nice bite, buddy. Here's this nummy toy to bite instead of my hand. Lindsay, you weren't kidding about Little Mr. Crocodile here."

"So, how was your date with Elliot?" Lindsay asked, picking up toys that had escaped the toy box.

"Fine."

"Merely fine?"

"Yeah, he took me to dinner, and then we walked around Temple Square for a bit."

"Hmm."

"What?"

"That sounds an awful lot like a hint to me."

"No, it wasn't. We had an enjoyable time talking."

Lindsay gave her sister a look. "Did Alisa and Caleb get into town okay?"

"Yes. I like Tom. He will be great for Alisa. You should have seen him sprint to get to her door before she could open it."

"Cute! And Caleb?"

"He's fine." Paige made a face.

"What does that face mean?"

"If you must know, he's giving me the cold shoulder, so there're no worries about me getting back with him."

"I wasn't worried about that," Lindsay said. "Though it wouldn't be a bad thing if you did. He's a much better catch now than when he was in high school."

"What?"

"Really? What were the two biggest things Mom and Dad objected to when he asked you to marry him? He wasn't LDS, and he had just joined the Marines. Now he's a commissioned officer and a young single LDS man. If they didn't know him at all, they'd be shoving you right at him."

"Well, even if they tried now, it wouldn't matter. It's apparent he's still angry. He made it clear my presence annoyed him the entire ride from the airport and when we stopped to get a bite to eat."

"I'm sorry, Paige. It's probably for the best all around. Maybe he'll stop being the standard for everyone you date."

"What are you talking about?"

Lindsay rolled her eyes. "You compare every guy you date to Caleb. Why do you think you're still single? It would take angelic intervention for you to consider anyone else."

"I'm dating Elliot."

"You're not exactly rushing him toward the altar."

"Right, I'm not. We haven't dated that long. But that doesn't mean I couldn't be—eventually."

"What's the problem?"

"I don't know. He's sort of boring, and I don't feel anything when I look at him."

"Boring? Sis, there is something to be said for the boring ones. They're the ones that usually bring home a steady paycheck and help change diapers at two in the morning."

"I know for a fact you don't find Brent boring. It's impossible to be around you two sometimes, and he makes you laugh all the time. But he also brings home a good paycheck, helps change diapers, and loves to tell dad jokes."

"The jokes are funnier when he tells them," Lindsay said, smiling. "So, what are you going to do about Caleb? He will be around a lot."

"I'm hoping at some point I can get him alone so I can talk to him. Maybe we can call a truce for Lise's sake. All I want is a chance to apologize to him. For everything. How I handled it and for breaking his heart."

"Good luck with that," Lindsay said. "Alisa's only got three weeks to pull this thing together. You won't have a lot of time for quiet interludes with anyone, let alone someone who doesn't want to talk to you."

"When did you get so wise? Aren't you supposed to be the younger sister?"

"Yes, but I'm an old married woman with kids, so I outrank you now."

"Whatever." She took a teasing swipe at her sister's arm.

The door to the garage opened, and Brent walked in. He threw his briefcase and portfolio on the floor. "Done! I'm done for the week. I'm going upstairs, getting the monkey suit off, getting into something more comfortable, and then I'm dragging my wife off to someplace without children. Is that okay with you, Paige?"

"Absolutely. I love hanging out with my boys," Paige said. "You guys go have fun, and we will be dinosaurs until Dinosaur Cameron goes to bed."

"Wonderful. Oh, did Caleb get in okay?"

"Yeah, they're over at their parents' right now with Tom."

"Heh. I'd like to be a fly on the wall over there," Brent said, loosening his tie. "I wonder who was more nervous—the twins or Tom?"

"They never had a very good opinion of our church. They did all they could to keep Caleb and Alisa out. Now both their children belong to it," Paige said. "I can tell you Ted's going to be the most upset. I'm sure he hoped to walk Lise down the aisle."

"Ouch. Yeah, wouldn't want to be them," Brent said, heading up the stairs to the second floor. "Be right back, honey, and then we can go."

"I wonder how they're treating Tom," Paige mused. "He's the one who baptized them into the Church. At least that's one thing they can't blame me for."

"I feel bad for them, for sure. Karen will have a lot more to say about it than Ted," Lindsay said. "I hope everyone will be okay."

Lindsay dusted her hands off on her jeans. "Talking to Caleb will be a good thing. You'll get whatever it is off your chest, and then you'll give other perfectly eligible men a chance."

"One day, I'll meet the man I want to marry, and I'm sure I'll have no doubt about it when I do. I just haven't met him yet."

"Oh, babe," Brent said, coming back down the stairs, ready to go. "I got a call from Becca this afternoon. She and Lucie still plan on coming up here for the summer and wondered if they could stay with us."

"Why can't your sisters stay at Mom and Dad's?" Lindsay asked.

"They said they want to be around the boys."

"The last time they were here, they were out 'til all hours of the night. They woke Cameron up too many times to count because they were so noisy coming in."

"All right, all right," Brent said. "It was just an idea. I'll tell them they can come over whenever they want, but they need to stay at Mom and Dad's."

"Thank you," Lindsay said. "I love your sisters, but they're almost worse than the boys."

"What are you going to be up to this summer, Paige?" Brent asked.

"I'm staying at Mom and Dad's. Alisa asked me to be the maid of honor, and being close will make getting to appointments easier."

"Do you think my sisters could go to church with you, Paige?" Brent asked. "They said they don't want to go to the family ward, and I don't blame them."

"That's fine. Warn them I won't be waiting around for them to get ready. Once I leave, they'll have to find their own way to church."

"I'll tell them."

Brent and Lindsay walked out the door, and for the first little while it was dinosaurs and mac and cheese and snuggles. Once the boys were in bed, Paige took a minute to sit down and take a deep breath. She hadn't planned on the day before being so emotionally charged when she had agreed to babysit for Brent and Lindsay. Now she felt exhausted. Paige considered texting Alisa, but she didn't want to make things worse for a possibly awkward situation.

In her mind's eye, Caleb's angry glance took her breath away. Ten years hadn't been near enough time to lessen his ire, apparently. She sighed. Perhaps Lindsay was right. Paige might view dating other men with a little more enthusiasm if she apologized to Caleb, telling him she wished things had gone differently. Right now, it was one more thing to keep her busy rather than something she enjoyed.

CHAPTER 5

Paige exhaled deeply before ringing the doorbell. It had been a very long time since she'd been inside the Watson home. The door opened, and Karen Watson stood there. She greeted Paige with a sour expression.

"Come in, Paige," she said as she stepped aside to let her in.

Paige walked into a very frosty setting. Alisa and Tom stood off to the side, talking to each other. Caleb stood near a picture window in the back of the room. Karen walked into the kitchen where Ted stood vigilantly over the snacks.

Paige looked around the room that had been so familiar a long time ago. It was more open. The Watsons had done some remodeling to open up the space. They had taken down a down a wall, making the family and living rooms a large great room that led into the kitchen. The decorations, furniture, and color palate were all brand new and so different from how it used to be. It was one more reminder to Paige how things and people had changed over the last ten years.

"Oh, you opened up a wall," Paige said, trying her hardest to keep her tone light. "I love how the family room opens up into the kitchen now."

"Thank you," Karen said. "We did it a few years ago."

"It looks lovely."

Karen said nothing further, and Ted looked disinclined to say anything himself.

Paige made her way over to where Alisa stood.

"I'm taking it things didn't go very well last night," Paige said, lowering her voice.

"No," Alisa said. Now that she stood near her best friend, she saw Alisa's eyes were red-rimmed and tired looking. Alisa took Paige by the hand and drew her back toward her old bedroom.

As soon as Alisa shut the door, she sat down on her bed.

"I expected too much," Alisa said, taking in a shuddering breath. "I mean, you know Caleb and I invited them out to our baptism. We wanted to include them in everything. We tried to make them understand why this was important to both of us. But even then, they weren't listening. They kept going on and on about cults and snooty, stuck-up hypocrites and naming off all these people. Getting engaged only made things worse."

"But you told them about temples, right?" Paige asked.

"Yes, right after Tom and I got engaged," Alisa said. "We called them together. Tom had been on a mission, so he'd be able to help explain if there was something they didn't understand. I think seeing him made them more mad because he was the one who baptized us. Mom kept suggesting he'd only done it to find a wife, or something weird like that. Then they really lost it when we told them we were getting married in the temple. They accused Tom of trying to exclude them from our wedding. They said I was going along with it because I was too brainwashed to fight him on it."

Tears dripped down her cheeks. Paige hugged Alisa.

"I'm sorry," Paige said. "This is really hard for people to understand when it's such an important event in most people's lives. But we can do a ring ceremony or something like that, so we can include them. No one says you can't do that."

"I appreciate that, Paige, but I don't know if that's going to help very much in this situation," Alisa said. "My parents are so angry right now. They haven't come to see us since we got baptized, and I'm worried they're going to be rude to Tom the whole time."

"I wish there was a way to help this situation," Paige said.

"You can't," Alisa said. "If they hated it here so much, why stay? If they hated their neighbors so much, why put up with it for the last twelve years? I mean, I kind of get where they're coming from a little. It's hard being the only ones on the street whose car isn't heading out to church at the same time as everyone else's on Sunday morning. And sometimes you'd find out about some event that happened. You hadn't been told a thing about it because it was only talked about at church. It's hard to feel a part of the neighborhood in situations like that. But that still doesn't mean they have to be rude to Tom. He doesn't represent the people who excluded them."

"Maybe they need a little time to warm up to him," Paige said. "It's easy to make the worst assumptions about people before you meet them. They'll have to see he's a good guy the more time he spends with them before the wedding."

"Maybe," Alisa said, though her tone didn't sound very hopeful.

"Let me talk to my mom," Paige said. "How about I plan a shower for you without the arctic breeze blowing through it?"

Alisa nodded. "I'd like that. See how many girls from high school we can get together at the last minute?"

"That would be a lot of fun."

Paige waited until Alisa dried her eyes and had taken a chance to breathe normally before they returned to the living room.

Tom managed a slight smile for Paige.

"I see you're still in one piece," Paige said, moving over to him.

"Not for lack of trying," he said, taking a furtive glance over at the Watsons.

Paige looked over at Caleb. There was a stony set to his jaw. His position near the window did not invite anyone to approach him. It was probably best.

"So tomorrow, do you guys want to come with me to my singles ward?" Paige asked. "It's quieter than the family ward. No competing with baby cries and toddler tantrums to hear the speakers."

“That sounds like fun,” Alisa said. “What do you think, babe?”

“I’m game. I’ve never been in a ward in Utah. Should be interesting.”

“Caleb doesn’t look like he’s in the mood for talking, so I’ll let you guys talk to him about it later.”

Alisa nodded.

Paige looked over toward the kitchen. Tom and Karen had busied themselves getting the engagement party put together. They pulled out delicate champagne glasses and cheap plastic tumblers.

“Is there anything I can help you with, Karen?” Paige said, approaching the kitchen again. She reached over to the box of champagne glasses to help arrange them on the table.

“I’d say you’ve done plenty already,” Karen said, moving to stand in front of the box and looking Paige in the eye.

“I’m not sure what you’re—”

“Don’t stand there and pretend to not know what I’m talking about. The least you could do is admit to the backhanded way you got them in the end.”

“Karen—”

“Mrs. Watson, thank you. I only allow my friends to call me Karen.”

Paige bit her lip. This change in Karen wasn’t totally unexpected, but the severity of her anger and vitriol took Paige by surprise. She held her breath, trying to come up with something to respond with. She understood why Karen was angry, but her children’s conversion had nothing to do with her. Alisa had mentioned the discussions, but even Paige didn’t get a call until after their baptism. Alisa and Caleb had surprised everyone. If you had asked Paige before that, she would have told anyone that the chance of them converting was about zero percent.

“No,” Caleb’s voice came up from behind her. “This isn’t Paige’s doing. I will not let you crucify her in front of us when she had nothing to do with it. She wasn’t even there when we were investigating it. Blame Lise and me if you’re going to blame anyone. We joined of our own free will. It might have happened sooner if things had turned out differently, but, well, they didn't, and it's done."

"That's right; stand up for her," Karen said. "You always did, even after she tore your heart out and threw it on the ground. We tried to warn you. And it happened exactly like we said it would." Karen glared at Paige.

What was Karen talking about? Suddenly the room seemed to get hotter. Paige's heart rate increased as she looked helplessly between Caleb and Karen. Caleb didn't look at her. He focused on his parents, but Paige wished she knew what Karen meant. Caleb had stood up for her after what she had put him through?

"I wouldn't have to stand up for her if you weren't taking your anger at Alisa and me out on her."

"Who else besides her is to blame? She couldn't go five minutes without talking about her religion around you. She always got her way and you let her. Never mind what your dad and I thought about any of it—what we tried to warn you against."

The realization hit Paige out of nowhere. They were talking about the night Caleb had proposed. Karen was obviously still angry. Caleb's expression didn't change a bit. Paige's head swam. She'd never been privy to the aftermath at the Watsons' that night. She'd nursed her own broken and hopeless heart. She hadn't considered what Caleb might have gone through or what his parents' reaction would be.

"Nothing would have changed what happened that night. She said no. That was the end of it. Talking badly about her didn't accomplish anything, and it didn't console me."

The blood rushing through her head roared in Paige's ears. The temperature in the room was becoming unbearable. He'd been so angry, so heartbroken, but he'd stopped his parents from bad-mouthing her. Even if he didn't fully understand her decision himself, he cared enough to stand up to them even though he hurt inside.

"All that heartbreak for nothing. If you had listened to us . . . We tried to tell you she would never go through with it because she'd want you to be one of them first. And we were right. This religion causes nothing but misery, but you and Alisa run headlong into it. And its rules are implacable, exclusionary. Some church of God that is. We're your parents, but yet you ask us to be okay with being excluded on a church's whim."

"You had no problem with asking Paige to marry against her religion at the time, just so it suited you. Now you're expecting the same thing from your own daughter. Paige's probably glad she turned me down, now that she can see how she would have been treated as part of this family."

Paige's heart beat so fast it threatened to explode.

"I need some fresh air. Excuse me." She turned and exited the house. She leaned her back against the garage door, trying to get herself under control. Paige struggled to pull in adequate breaths and tears pooled in her eyes.

The maelstrom of feelings was more intense than she expected. Caleb's quick defense of her against his parents had her heart skipping beats. Paige had been perfectly capable of handling Karen on her own. She'd enough experience with entitled parents of elementary school kids to know how to handle a situation like that, but Karen's vehemence had surprised her. Caleb didn't make her handle it alone. She recognized she shouldn't read into it too much. That was hard because it was the type of sweet and heroic thing the Caleb from ten years ago loved doing for her. He was always quick to come to her rescue, like some danger-seeking knight in shining armor.

Alisa followed her out to the front of the house. She came up to Paige and rubbed her arms. She, too, had tears in her eyes.

"That's the last time I ever show up early to anything," Paige said, wiping away tears that threatened to fall. "She really doesn't honestly understand. Walking away from Caleb that night was the hardest thing I've ever done in my life. I'm not saying I was right, but you'd think your mom would have thought it was better for the both of us."

"All my mom understands is that you broke Caleb's heart that night, and all because of the Church," Alisa said, hugging herself. She leaned against the garage door next to Paige. "I can't stand all this anger. It's not like we've separated ourselves from them or they're not allowed in our lives anymore. We do things a little differently than them. What's so wrong with that? And Tom's a great guy. Does it really matter that much if he's religious? Wouldn't they want me to be with a good guy?"

Paige hugged Alisa. “I’m so sorry,” Paige said. “All of this should be about you and Tom.”

“It’s not your fault. You were just another target she could take aim at. There wasn’t much more she could say to us after last night. I hope one day she understands so she’s not so bitter.”

Tom peeked his head around the corner where the two women stood. “Hi,” he said. “Are you guys okay?”

“No, but we will be,” Alisa said, walking over to him and wrapping her arms around him. “We should have eloped. Las Vegas has a temple.”

They all laughed. “Not sure it works like a Chapel O’ Love,” he said. “They sent me out here because she’s agreed to be on her best behavior the rest of the party.”

“Sounds like that’s as good as it will get,” Alisa said. “Are you coming back in with us?”

“Yes. Like I said, this is about you and Tom, and I won’t ruin it by letting my emotions get the better of me.”

They walked back in the door. Karen was putting out a balloon arch she’d brought in from the garage. Paige grabbed the other side and tied it down across from where Karen was tying her end. She kept busy, silently helping Karen with setting up the snack and present tables as people gradually arrived. Ted stood up and called for attention by tapping a knife on his champagne glass when the room had filled to near capacity.

“Everyone, could I have your attention, please?” Ted said over the noise of the gathering.

He held up a champagne flute and indicated to a table near the kitchen.

“I’d like everyone to join us in a toast. Champagne, or sparkling apple cider for the teetotalers.” The crowd chuckled.

“Friends and neighbors, in a few short weeks my daughter, Alisa, has chosen to marry Tom Fields, a captain in the U.S. Marines. He promised me he will love her and take care of her as much or more than her mother and I have. We hold him to that promise. Though we may not understand about temples and things, the one thing we do understand is love and devotion. Alisa, may Tom endeavor to deserve you. Tom, may you take care of our little girl. Karen and I wish you both a long life together." Ted's voice cracked. "And all the happiness you deserve. To the engaged couple—Tom and Alisa."

Ted raised his glass and said, "Cheers." Everyone followed suit. Ted downed the champagne in one big gulp. Karen sipped at hers, but she acted like the taste didn't appeal to her.

Tom and Alisa hugged the Watsons before wandering off to mingle with their guests.

Paige looked around. She didn't see Caleb anywhere in the room. She found him in the backyard and watched him through the big picture window. She nearly joined him but held herself back. The look he had given her yesterday kept her away.

He turned to look at her as if sensing her stare on his back. His face was unreadable. There was sadness there and something else that eluded her. Her breath quickened when she remembered how he had stood up for her against his mother, and she turned to go back to the party.

Many of their longtime neighbors were there to congratulate the engaged couple. Caleb had come back inside and made himself sociable. Paige found him cornered by their oldest neighbor, Sister Montez.

"I can't believe the boy who used to drop papers off on my porch is this man before me," she said. "And still not married?"

"No, ma'am."

She looked over at Paige as she came a little too close to avoid being drawn into the conversation. Sister Montez reached out and took Paige's hand, pulling her closer into the trio.

"You know, you two would have made a beautiful couple, but I suppose that's the way life is sometimes," she said, patting Paige's hand. Paige and Caleb looked at each other. Paige averted her gaze, her cheeks blazing.

"Thanks, Sister Montez," Paige said. "Life takes us in different directions sometimes. I'm a schoolteacher in West Jordan, and Caleb's a pilot for the Marines."

“It’s not too late,” Sister Montez said. “You should snatch up this handsome young man before another girl gets there first.”

Paige laughed nervously. “I don’t think he wants to be ‘snatched up,’ ” Paige said. “But it’s kind of you to look out for the both of us. I think we’ll find who we’re looking for when the time is right.”

“Exactly so, my dear,” Sister Montez said. “Sometimes it takes a little time and patience with the Lord’s timetable to lead us to where He wants us. I’m sure He knows exactly what you both need and is leading you to it.” If Sister Montez expected a reaction out of either, she didn’t get it. Paige didn’t know what to say, and Caleb stood there with a smile plastered on his face.

Sister Montez rubbed Caleb’s arm. “I think I’ll go sample those sandwiches your mother made.”

Paige hurried to find Alisa without giving Caleb a second glance. Too much feeling buzzed around her from today and what Sister Montez had said about the Lord leading them where He wanted them wasn’t helping. The last thing she wanted was for Caleb to clue in to her addled emotions.

Chapter 6

Paige stayed to help clean up after the party was over and then walked down the sidewalk to her parents' house.

"Rough day?" her dad said as he sat on the porch whittling a piece of wood.

"You might say that," she replied, sitting down next to him.

"Karen give you an earful?"

"She handed out individually tied-up packages of 'earful' for everyone there but Ted," Paige said, sighing.

"How do the twins look?"

"Alisa looks on cloud nine. She's head over heels for Tom, and he's a great guy. I think they'll be very happy together."

"And Caleb?"

"Oh, he's looking good too. He's taller than I remembered him."

"Taller? The kid's in the Marines for nearly a decade, and he only got taller?"

"He's not a gawky teenager anymore, if that's what you're trying to get at, Dad," Paige said. She looked away from him so he wouldn't see the blush in her cheeks.

"And you've done a lot of growing up yourself," he said, patting her on the knee. "He couldn't have failed to notice that."

"It doesn't matter," she answered. "He's made it very clear that he merely tolerates my presence. I'm not sure how I will get through the upcoming weeks with him acting like the mere sight of me disgusts him."

"His loss if he can't let go of his anger," Willy said. "Besides, you're different people now. He can be stand-offish all he wants because it won't matter after a few weeks. You both have careers that keep you busy. When he goes back home, you'll both go back to doing what you were doing. Get through the wedding. Don't overthink it. You staying the night?"

"Yeah, I'll move in with you guys for the next few weeks," she said, standing up. "Mom's idea. It will be better if I'm right here so Alisa and I can up and leave when we need to."

"What about church?" Willy asked.

"It's only once a week," Paige said. "I'll probably still make the drive down to my ward. It'll be nice to take the Sunday drive with everyone."

"Wonderful plan," he replied. "Glad you'll be around. Mom and I miss you girls sometimes."

"Good night, Dad. I'll see you tomorrow morning." She stood up and turned to kiss her father on his head.

"Go on"—he waved at her—"go to bed."

Sleep sounded amazing after what had happened today. All the drama wore her out. She couldn't imagine what it had been like for the twins, let alone Tom. He'd willingly stepped into the lion's den for the woman he loved. Caleb, too, had stood up for *her*, defending her against his mother. But he wasn't in love with her. His defense just made him a decent guy, not someone who still had feelings for her. And what did she have? She couldn't deny the butterflies she had every time she looked at him, but a brief stab of guilt would dampen those flutterings. Next chance that presented itself, she'd talk to him. She'd clear the air, then they'd both move on. Maybe she'd move on with Elliot. Doubtful, but stranger, more unlikely things might happen.

She was about to go to sleep when she got a text notification.

I forgot to tell you after all the craziness
Mom's made us an appointment at Phillipe's looking at wedding dresses.
Dad's taking Tom out to lunch, but Caleb's coming with us.
I hope that's okay.

Sweetie, this is your wedding—
you can invite whoever you want to whatever you want.
I promise to be on my best behavior if he is.

Okay, meet us there at 10am.
I'm slowly getting excited again.

I'll be there!

Yet another day in Caleb's company. She hoped this next time he'd be more relaxed than he had been. Didn't he realize every time he was a jerk or made a snide comment to Paige, he wounded his sister? There was already enough strife going on in the Watson home. He didn't need to add more.

Paige lay there in the dark. Her stomach and chest clenched as she remembered the night Caleb proposed to her. She recalled standing on the steps of the house as he pulled the ring box out of his pocket that hot graduation night. He'd tried to kneel in front of her to ask her. He hadn't even finished his first sentence before she shook her head and said, "I can't!" His face had gone from elated to broken in mere seconds.

"We talked about this already," Paige pleaded. "I've wanted a forever family my entire life. I can only do that if I marry in the temple. I can only do that if the person I marry is a faithful member of my church. You're not a member, so I can't marry you."

"Then I'll get baptized," Caleb said. "We'll do it your way."

"How many days ago was it you were telling me you wouldn't because your mom and dad wouldn't like it?"

"Yeah, well, I didn't think you'd turn me down because of it. We still love each other, right? Or am I the only one now? Then fine, I'll get baptized. We'll get married, and you can come with me before I leave for the Marines."

"It doesn't work like that. It shouldn't work like that," Paige cried. "You get baptized because you honestly feel this is the church for you. You don't get baptized because you want to be with me."

"Then I don't know what you want from me," he said, frustrated. "You say you won't marry me because I won't get baptized; then you say I can't get baptized. Which one is it?"

"Both, unless you really, truly choose to join the Church for you."

"All I want to do is marry you. I don't care where or how. I just want to be with you. You're the one giving out ultimatums. Making this harder than it needs to be."

"I'm not trying to," she declared, tears dripping out of her eyes. "You shouldn't join my church just because I said so."

"My parents were right," Caleb replied. "You don't think I'm good enough for you, for your family." The stubbornness set his jaw.

"No!" she cried. "We just have different ideas on some very important things. It would make marriage harder."

"That's your parents talking. Did you give any thought about how I would feel about this? Do you even care? It's always been your way or the highway, hasn't it, Paige?"

"That's not it, Caleb. I love you so much. It's tearing me up inside that I have to say no. I wish I could make you understand."

"Me too. Because you're doing a really crappy job so far. Paige, please. Come with me. We'll make it work. We love each other."

She shook her head. "I can't. It wouldn't be fair to either of us. I want us to be together forever, not just in this life. I want it to be with you. But I will not try to force you to believe what I want you to believe. You'd resent me if I tried."

"You don't know what I'd do because you're not giving me the chance to show you. And now time is running out. I leave for boot camp in a little over a month. I'd ask you to follow me, but I know you won't without us being married."

"I'm so sorry, Caleb," she sobbed. "I wish things were different." She hugged herself, trying not to fall apart.

"Fine. You've made your choice," Caleb said, standing as stiff as a statue. "But don't you dare tell me you love me again because it's not true. People who care for each other work it out, and you don't want to work it out."

He turned and walked down the sidewalk toward his house. Paige sat on the steps and bawled her eyes out. He didn't shed a single tear. And he was the one accusing her of not loving him. Her heart splintered into a thousand tiny pieces. She loved him more than he realized, but she'd never be able to convince him of that. When he left for the Marines, she may never see him again. How was she going to explain this to Alisa?

Paige ran into the house and threw herself into bed, ignoring the knocks that came at her door. She turned over and cried herself to sleep that night.

Paige's tears leaked out of the sides of her eyes. Even now, the way she tried to explain to Caleb why she couldn't marry him made her cringe. It made her sound selfish, stuck up, and judgmental. All she had been trying to do was marry the way the Lord had said would make both people the happiest. She pondered what might have happened if she had said yes to him that night, come what may. Would they still be happy with each other? They both had been so young. What would they have known about making a marriage work?

CHAPTER 7

Paige paced back and forth in front of the fitting platform while Caleb sat sprawled out in an armchair, lying back. In the last hour at the dress shop, Alisa had come out in a dress that looked like a nightgown, one where the lace of the upper bodice and sleeves was so sheer, she'd never get away with it in the temple, and one that looked like she was going to a Renaissance festival. It was not looking good.

Alisa came around the corner in a meringue fluff with sleeves so high they almost hid the sides of her head. Paige ran up and adjusted them, making them appear more like cotton balls than fabric blinders.

"Who picked this one?" Paige asked.

"Mom," Alisa said, grimacing.

"It's not 1989 anymore," Paige quickly whispered to Alisa before Karen came around the corner.

"Oh, I love it. You look so beautiful," Karen gushed.

"No, she doesn't," Caleb said, sitting up with a look of disgust on his face. "That's a terrible dress, Mom."

"She's the one insisting on long sleeves for a summer wedding. That limits the number of dresses."

"You really want long sleeves?" Paige asked Alisa.

"I heard long sleeves are a requirement in the temple."

"They are, but they have sleeve inserts you can attach to a short or cap sleeve on the dress," Paige said.

"Really? I've spent an hour in hideous dresses because I didn't know that?"

Paige giggled. "You didn't ask me about it, did you? You asked a boy, and they don't know stuff like that."

"Thankfully," Caleb said.

"Get me out of this thing. I want to see some dresses with short sleeves," Alisa declared as she headed back to the dressing room.

Caleb stood up and walked with Paige to the racks of dresses. "No. No. Nope. Gross. What in the—? Here's one. And this one."

"Are you making sure you're picking her size out of those?"

"Of course," he said, looking offended, but she saw him put back one dress for the right size.

"Since when did you become an expert on wedding dresses?" Paige asked, picking out a few of her favorites.

"My sister, whom I love very much, is getting married to my best friend," he said. "She needs to look spectacular."

"Aww, that's so nice of you," Paige said.

"Thanks," Caleb said, giving her a partial smile. Paige's stomach did a flip. It was the first time since he'd been back that the smirky smile she loved so much had made an appearance. And directed at her. They took the dresses to Alisa's fitting room.

"Mom, I told you. The dress has to have a little bit of sleeve on it," she said from behind the door.

"It's such a ridiculous stipulation," Karen said. "This mermaid is perfectly lovely. Couldn't you at least try it on?"

"Mom, it doesn't even have shoulder straps."

"Knock, knock," Paige said, cracking the door open. "Caleb and I found a few you might like."

"You and Caleb?" Alisa asked.

"Ask him," she said.

"I have great taste. I'll bet you pick one of my dresses," Caleb said.

"Yeah, right," Paige said, shaking her head. "He may be your beloved brother, but he is only a boy."

"Are you willing to bet I make you eat your words?"

"Bet what?"

"Whoever's dress doesn't get picked pays for ice cream at Leatherby's later," he said, a glint in his eye. She looked into his hazel eyes and couldn't help the smile that played at the corners of her mouth. This was classic Caleb from back in the day as well. Anytime he could, he'd make the littlest things a competition and it was usually over the silliest things. Paige loved it.

"You've got yourself a bet," she said. He walked off. Paige turned around to see Alisa laughing.

"You guys are so ridiculous," she said.

"He started it," Paige said though both friends smiled. Challenges like this from Caleb was one of the things that she loved about being around him in high school. Part of it was he always made her laugh, but part of it was he didn't make things easy for her. She liked feeling like she could one-up him. There were times when she felt like smacking him because he could be so frustrating, but that was all part of his charm.

She went back into the waiting area and found Caleb looking on a rack of veils.

“Find anything interesting?” she asked.

He shrugged his shoulders. “A couple, but when she picks my dress, then I’ll pick one.”

“You take a great interest in her wedding plans. It’s sweet,” Paige said. She was glad it was one thing that hadn’t changed about him. In high school, as much as he cared for Paige, Caleb was always very loving towards his twin and mindful of her needs. Paige knew Alisa didn’t think twice about taking care of Caleb. Seemed Caleb felt the same about Alisa even as adults.

“When they were getting ready to send me to Camp Pendleton after boot camp,” he said, “I planned on going all by myself, but Alisa insisted on coming with me. She’s followed me around the country every time I got stationed somewhere, supporting me in my career, and got her own started in the meantime. That means a lot to me. She deserves a wedding that goes off without too many hitches.”

“I’m sure she couldn’t ask for a more loving or helpful little brother,” Paige smirked.

Caleb glanced at her, caught her smirk and folded his arms.

“You two really can’t help yourselves, can you?”

“I’m surprised a big, buff soldier like you would still let it get to him.”

“A big, buff officer, thank you very much. I worked my butt off for that commission, I’ll have you know.”

“I’m sure you did,” Paige said, leaning back against the wall. “You were always very determined when you wanted something.”

“Determined,” he mused, looking at her with mischief in his eyes. “I guess that’s a good word for it. I am pretty single-minded when I see something I want.”

Paige smiled but felt a blush creeping into her cheeks. He’d proven in the past how single-minded he was when he wanted something. “Well, it’s good you’re willing to help Alisa. Seems most brothers are there for the party. The rest of the time they stay out of the way.”

“Not me,” Caleb said. “I’m excited for her and Tom.”

"Reminds me of something cute that happened last week. I had a student named Caleb in my class this last year. He was a handful, but so sweet. He didn't want to stay home over the summer and take care of his baby sister. But I told him he needed to be a big helper like my friend, Big Caleb. I told him you were always helping people because that's what soldiers do."

"You called me 'Big Caleb?'"

Paige nodded, biting her lip to keep from grinning.

Caleb smiled a little.

"The fact you were a soldier didn't seem to impress him as much as whether you had fired a gun," Paige said.

Caleb laughed. Paige was unable to hide her smile now.

"Well?"

"Well, what?"

"Have you ever fired a gun?"

"I'm a Marine," he said. "Of course I've fired a gun."

Paige paused. She remembered the day before and his help with his mother. No matter what had happened between them in the past, it was a generous thing for him to do. If she wanted to start the process of burying the hatchet, then gratitude usually was a good first step.

"Caleb, I'd like to thank you for yesterday," Paige said, taking in a deep breath. "You didn't have to, and I was going to defend myself, but she caught me off guard. I just wanted to let you know I appreciated it."

He looked at her. "You're welcome. You didn't deserve that, and it had already been a rough twenty-four hours. I'm sorry she thought she could talk to you like that."

Paige looked at her feet. "Well, in a way, I understand why she's upset. It's difficult to accept that your children are following a different path than you'd always planned for them. When I was on my mission, we had a couple of new converts who dealt with that."

"What did they do?" he asked.

"We asked them to pray for their family members that their hearts would be softened," Paige said. "Sometimes it was more a matter of accepting the membership in the Church rather than understanding the reasons for joining."

Caleb sighed. "Alisa and I have spent lots of time doing that. It affects Alisa most of all, because she wants Mom and Dad to understand even if they don't like it." He stopped what he was doing. "Australia, huh?"

Paige faced him, her face beaming. "Yes. It was wonderful. I wanted to stay longer. I even put in for an extension, but they sent me home on time anyway. It's okay, though. I got my teacher's recertification and jumped right into working. I started out in kindergarten and then third grade."

"You, teaching rugrats," Caleb said, smirking. "It suits you."

"Just like it's hard for me to imagine you doing anything other than flying planes," she said.

"It is a rush," he said.

Caleb had been scanning the racks of veils and combs during their conversation.

He looked over at Paige. "What do you think of this one?"

He had pulled down a cream-colored veil with a delicate leaf and rhinestone tiara.

"Oh, that is pretty," she said.

"May I?" he said, holding up the tiara.

Paige bent down, though with their height difference it was hardly necessary. He placed it on her head. She looked at herself in the mirror on the wall behind them. The cream-colored tulle set off the creaminess of her skin and made the red of her hair stand out more.

The rhinestones sparkled brightly in the store lights. She felt like a princess, and standing behind her was the man who was once her Prince Charming, staring at her in the mirror. The lines of his face had softened while she inspected the veil.

Paige's cheeks burned as she took the tiara off and handed it back to him. "I think if she picks a cream-colored gown, then it would be perfect."

He took the tiara back from her without taking his eyes from her. He didn't say anything, and she found it hard to look away.

The sound of Karen's voice brought Paige back to reality. "Step carefully, baby, this one has an extra-long train."

Alisa stepped out onto the fitting platform and gasped. The lace gown had short sleeves, a tight-fitting bodice, and flared at the knee. She turned to examine all the angles. Tears sprouted from her eyes, and Paige rushed up to her friend and hugged her. It wasn't one of her choices.

"I love it," Alisa said, looking from Paige to Caleb.

"You're sure you don't want to try on any others?" Karen asked.

"No. This is the one."

"Okay. Dress has been found," Karen said with a tired sigh. "Now check that off the three hundred other things on the to-do list before the wedding day."

Caleb's breath tickled Paige's neck as he leaned over slightly said, "Someone's paying for ice cream."

CHAPTER 8

Paige drove Caleb, Alisa, and Tom south toward the ice cream parlor. They had taken off to get their treat after dropping Karen off at the Watsons' and rescuing Tom from Mr. Watson. Caleb sat in the passenger seat, while the engaged couple sat in the back. Paige tried not letting his close proximity get her too excited. Something had sparked between them at the bridal shop. She wondered what it meant. Caleb was acting more normal, more relaxed. And his teasing sense of humor had finally resurfaced. A pleasant warmth radiated between them, sitting so close together.

Caleb turned to Paige. "I can pay for this. It's not really that big a deal."

"Fair is fair," Paige replied, glancing at Caleb. "I lost, so I'm paying."

"What do you mean, you lost?" Tom questioned.

"I made a bet with Paige that Alisa would pick a dress I chose for her. The loser would pay for ice cream at Leatherby's."

"It's so funny to see you guys still so competitive," Alisa said, chuckling.

"What is Leatherby's? I don't think they have those in California or South Carolina," Tom said.

"It's a local ice cream parlor. People call it a Utah institution because it's been around a long time," Paige answered. "That's only one reason, though. Leatherby's is awesome.

Their ice cream is outstanding. They serve up huge portions, and when I say huge, I mean massive. So, don't let your eyes get bigger than your stomach."

"You underestimate a Marine's appetite."

"Okay. Giving you fair warning. It's your stomachache later." Paige laughed. "Lise, we're sharing the small banana split like usual, right?"

"Yes. I need to slow down. They're going to have to take out my dress if I'm not careful."

They pulled up to an old building. "The outside's not very impressive," Tom stated.

"The aesthetic is outdated, but the ice cream is still amazing."

Things had changed little since high school. The inside was cramped, jammed with parlor tables and chairs. Other than the occasional pop of colored tile, the beige tiling and yellowing order signs spoke of the age of the place. They squeezed together at the small parlor table.

Caleb and Tom stretched out as soon as the server took their orders.

"Tom, you're a brave man. You're getting the Daddy Doug's Banana Special?" Paige asked.

"What?" Tom asked.

"You'll find out soon enough," Paige said, shaking her head.

"Speaking of daddies, how did your lunch go with my dad?" Alisa asked.

"Um, it went okay," Tom said. "He was at least civil rather than outright hostile."

Alisa took his hand in hers. "That's an improvement."

"Yeah," he said, his face scrunched up a little. "He defined what his expectations for being your husband were. I respect that. If we have a daughter, I'll probably do the same thing. I think it helped him feel better about everything because he explained it to me."

The server came with a tray stacked with their orders. When she set Tom's order in front of him, he leaned back in his chair a little, his eyes wide. The enormous dish had three baseball-sized scoops of chocolate, vanilla, and strawberry ice cream that smothered two lengths of banana. They had drowned all of it in caramel and chocolate sauces with pineapple topping. Precariously balanced on top was another baseball-sized serving of whipped cream, splashed with almonds and two bright maraschino cherries on top.

"You can say it," he responded, looking at everyone.

"Nope," Caleb replied. "No need. Just hike up a pant leg and dig in."

"I'd almost forgotten how good the banana splits are here," Alisa said as she took her first bite.

"So good I got in trouble with my dad that first summer you guys moved here. We drove his car down here once a week. Remember that?" Paige asked.

"Oh, is that why your dad grounded you for a while?"

"Yup, he couldn't figure out why he was constantly needing to fill the car with gas. Lindsay tattled on me. I wouldn't take her with us, and she got mad and told my dad. Brat."

Alisa laughed.

"Did you two get into trouble a lot as teens?" Tom asked.

The women shook their heads and pointed to Caleb.

Tom laughed. "Dude, you're so strait-laced sometimes. It's hard to believe you ever got into trouble."

"Oh, he got into trouble a lot, and he would nearly drag us down with him. I was the smarty-pants, and he was his version of a bad boy," Paige replied.

"He had this pair of skinny jeans. He wore them any chance he could get. He'd have to lie down on his bed to pull them on because they were so tight." Alisa snorted she was laughing so hard.

"My favorite was that black jean jacket and hoodie combo," Paige added.

"You liked that?" Caleb asked. "My mom used to complain it smelled."

Paige blushed. "It smelled like you." She remembered she'd steal it any chance she'd get when he'd take it off, just so she could wrap herself up in it. It was almost like being hugged by him, but not quite.

"These two argued about the dumbest stuff," Alisa said. "Caleb did it on purpose."

"What?" Paige demanded, shocked.

"You loved to argue, so I'd start disagreeing with everything you said just to see how far I could take it. She spent an entire day trying to convince me why Smarties were far superior to Sweetarts."

"Did she convince you?" Tom smirked.

"No, because I already like Smarties better than Sweetarts, but she didn't know that."

Everyone laughed.

"That was around Valentine's, right? Do you remember the time Caleb dared you to throw a Valentine's card paper airplane at Mr. Jenkins? Paige thought it wouldn't be a big deal because his back was to the class," Alisa said.

"He turned around at the wrong time. If he hadn't been wearing his glasses, I would have gotten him in the eye."

"Your aim was impressive," Caleb responded.

"Yeah, and he almost caught me."

"But he didn't." Caleb smirked.

"I remember how the vein in his forehead sort of popped out as he tried to find out who it was," Alisa said, giggling.

"Lucky for me, I was friends with most everyone in the class. Caleb liked to dare me to do stuff like that. I'm not sure how I stayed out of trouble."

"It's because you're smart and talked your way out of almost anything," Caleb said. "All the teachers took anything you said at face value; you were such a goodie-two-shoes. Teacher's pet."

"Sort of ironic, considering I'm a teacher myself now," Paige replied.

"I love hearing all these stories about you guys in high school," Tom said. "Caleb's definitely different from what I imagined him, but then again, he's not so different."

"It was a very fun and interesting time in our lives," Caleb said. "Throw in my best friend at the time, Brent Groves, and there were shenanigans. He and I spent a lot of time in detention cleaning white boards."

"So, Paige, is that why you turned this fool down? Couldn't be seen hanging out with the hooligans?"

The table went silent. Paige put her chin against her chest and glanced over at Caleb. His face was an emotionless granite mask.

Alisa stood up and grabbed Tom by the hand. "Let's go outside for a second. We'll be right back."

Paige didn't know what to say, and Caleb seemed disinclined to speak. An oppressive heaviness rolled in like a fog. Paige's mind roiled with what to do or say. She thought about her vow to apologize to Caleb before he returned to South Carolina. They were alone, but Alisa and Tom could come back at any time. She'd hate to be in the middle of that conversation when they came back. She glanced at him again and took in a breath to say something. A sinking feeling in her stomach deflated the effort, and she looked away to see where Alisa and Tom went. They stood outside talking to each other. Her fingers weaved in and out of each other under the table. Should she say something?

"I was sure Lise had told him," Paige mumbled.

"Sometimes I wonder if his brain bothers to engage before his mouth does," he said, staring at his unfinished ice cream.

"I really like Tom," Paige said, desperate to keep the conversation going. The silence was agony.

"He is a good guy, most of the time," Caleb answered.

"He's lucky he's getting Alisa," Paige said, giving Caleb a slight smile. "She's already used to living the military lifestyle. It won't be much of a change for her."

"It's a big transition for those not used to it. A lot of the young military wives don't know what to do with themselves. Some of them lay around and do nothing, spending their husband's paychecks," he stated. "It made me think of how much you depended on your parents. Not sure how well you would have adjusted to living independently of them."

"Excuse me?"

"A strong sense of independence seems to be the deciding factor if someone makes a good military spouse," he said, finally looking at her. "You need to make decisions on your own without always consulting your parents about everything."

"I have no idea what you're talking about," Paige bristled. "You obviously don't know me anymore. I don't depend on them at all, except as part of my family. Everything I've accomplished I did on my own, without them deciding for me or helping me financially. I paid my own way through college *and* my mission. I live on my own. I live on a budget. I own my car outright, and I have a full-time job with a skill set and years of experience."

"That's very nice," he replied. Was he being sarcastic?

"If I wanted to sit around and do nothing but spend my spouse's money, then I'd marry the lawyer I'm dating. He'd set me up nicely for the rest of our lives," she said, standing up so quickly she almost tipped her chair over. "Dependent on my parents. Nice, Caleb."

She paid for their ice cream and walked out the door without looking back.

"I'll be waiting for you guys in the car," she said, blood boiling as she brushed past a surprised Alisa and Tom. She got in her car and seethed until the rest of them joined her.

Alisa and Tom chatted in the back seat as they drove home. Paige kept her eyes on the road and her mouth shut. She didn't want to say something in front of Alisa she would regret. This was Alisa's time to shine, and Paige refused to tarnish that because her brother was a jerk.

CHAPTER 9

Sunday morning Paige drove up to Groves' house. The Groves had done little to change their house on the outside. It was a beige brick rambler with a perfectly mowed lawn and large boxy bushes that flanked the front porch. She wondered briefly if they had done any changes to the inside like the Watsons had. She didn't want to find out. Loretta was a sweet lady, but she could talk the ear off of a dog.

The nostalgia overload never seemed to end since she'd come back to Bountiful. Brent had been Caleb's best friend in high school. The four of them—Alisa, Caleb, Paige, and Brent—had ping-ponged between the Watson, Ellis, and Groves' houses throughout the last half of high school. Now Brent was her brother-in-law. Paige knew first-hand, because of those years in high school, he was perfect for Lindsay, and he was a good guy. She wasn't sure she could say the same for his sisters, Becca and Lucie.

Brent's sisters were as close as two sisters could be. Becca, though she was the younger of the two, was definitely the dominant personality. Lucie went along with whatever her sister did. When they were younger, they were nuisances, always trying to insert themselves in whatever Paige's little group was doing. Even though they had graduated from high school, things had changed very little for them. They drove Lindsay crazy. They loved their nephews to pieces, but they weren't very aware of things like naptimes or house rules or common courtesy.

Paige had made sure she'd texted Becca a half hour early so they wouldn't be late. It was still another twenty-minute drive to West Jordan. Brent's sisters, even at twenty and nineteen, would have made them late if Paige hadn't.

The door to the house opened, and the two girls ran and got in the car. They might have been twins, except Lucie's sweetheart-shaped face was a contrast to her sister's oval face. They both had the same color of blonde hair and wore similar styles.

"Hi, Paige!" Becca exclaimed, as she climbed into the seat behind Paige. Lucie took the front seat.

"It's been a super long time since we saw you. You look all grown up," Becca declared.

"That's because I am," Paige said, smiling. "What are you two doing now?"

"We're both going to school down in Provo," Becca replied. "I'm at Bon Losee, and Lucie's at BYU."

"Oh, you're studying to be a beautician, Becca?"

"Yes, I'm going to be the best colorist in the state," Becca said. "I can't wait to graduate. Lucie's still got another year and a half." Becca laughed like that was the funniest thing ever. Her laugh was loud and harsh.

"You guys dating anyone?"

"Me? No. The boys down in Provo are so stupid. They think they own the earth or something, because the girls outnumber them two to one. I'm not chasing after some stupid boy. Unlike Lucie. Tell her, Lucie."

Lucie gave Paige a shy smile. "I'm waiting for Brad Wilcox. He's on his mission in Alabama."

"Oh, you have a man," Paige replied. "How much longer until he comes home?"

"Another fourteen months," Lucie said, sighing.

"It'll go by fast," Paige said, reaching over and squeezing Lucie's hand. "One day I was arriving in Australia on my mission. Then the next day, it seemed, I was coming back home."

"I hope it goes by fast. Fourteen months seems like such a long time," Lucie said.

"So, Paige, are you dating anyone?" Becca asked.

"I am," Paige answered. "His name is Elliot. You'll probably meet him today. He goes to my ward."

"Oh, is he hot? What does he do for a living?" Becca asked.

"I think he's handsome, so I guess you could say he's *hot*. You can judge for yourself when you meet him. And he works as a lawyer for a firm in Salt Lake."

"A lawyer!" Becca said, whistling. "Why aren't you engaged to him yet?"

"We're getting to know each other," Paige said. "We're in no hurry."

"If you say so," Becca said, grimacing. "I'd love to marry a lawyer."

"You said you wanted to marry a rancher so you could own horses," Lucie said.

"I would marry a rancher. But we don't know any ranchers. We don't even know anyone who knows a rancher," Becca replied. "So, I'll save my pennies and buy my own property and my own horses."

"That's the spirit, Becca," Paige said. "You don't need a man for that. If you're the best colorist in the state, then you'll make plenty of your own money to buy what you want."

"You have to have a man if you want kids," Lucie stated.

"That's true," Paige said.

They pulled up to the church building. Paige stepped out of her car to see Caleb, Tom and Alisa walking up the sidewalk to her car.

"Holy buckets, who is that?" Becca asked. Paige followed her line of sight straight to Caleb.

"The one holding hands with Alisa is her fiancé, Tom. And the other one is Caleb."

"It is?" Becca practically shouted. "Wow, now that's what I call hot."

When the trio arrived, Paige said, "You guys remember Brent's little sisters, Becca and Lucie?"

"Sure," Alisa said. "You two are not in elementary school anymore, are you?"

Becca scoffed. "We haven't been in elementary school for forever. So, you're Tom? Alisa is so lucky," she said, shaking Tom's hand. Becca turned to Caleb, looking up at him through her lashes. "It seems like it's been forever since we saw you, Caleb. You remember us, right?"

"Yes. You guys have grown up, haven't you?" Caleb said, addressing Becca with his famous crooked grin.

"Want to get some seats before there aren't any?" Paige said, gritting her teeth.

Men! It would just figure he'd head straight for the nineteen-year-old, Paige thought. It only got worse once they got inside the chapel. Becca maneuvered herself to sit next to Caleb. Paige tried to tune out their conversation and Becca's giggles. She folded her arms as if that would hold back her irritation. When sacrament meeting was over, Elliot approached her. He pulled her into a quick hug.

"Elliot, you remember me telling you about my friend, Alisa," Paige said. Elliot hovered next to Paige nearly hip to hip as he shook Alisa and then Tom's hands. "And this is her fiancé, Tom."

"Yes, you're in the Marines, right, Tom?" Elliot asked.

"Yes, me and this lunkhead back here," Tom said, pointing to Caleb. "We're stationed at the same base. That's how I met Alisa."

"That's fantastic. Let me congratulate you, then, on your upcoming marriage."

"The lunkhead in the back is Alisa's brother, Caleb," Paige said. He turned from something Becca was saying after hearing his name spoken. His eyes immediately zeroed in on Elliot's proximity to Paige.

"Yes, nice to meet you," Caleb said, sticking his hand out to Elliot. Paige watched as Caleb's hand muscles flexed, shaking Elliot's. She rolled her eyes. "I'm sorry. I missed your name."

"My name's Elliot Fraser," he said, putting a hand around to the small of Paige's back. "Paige and I are dating."

"He's the lawyer," Paige said, trying to look innocent.

Caleb's eyes flicked to Paige's for a moment, a grimace spreading across his face before Becca tugged on his dress shirt.

"I have the funniest thing to tell you," she said.

Paige's stomach unknotted when Caleb turned around. She almost slapped Elliot's hand from around her waist. He didn't need to be territorial with Caleb around, and it bothered her he was being so physical.

"Come on, let's go to Sunday School," Paige stated. Paige grabbed Elliot's hand and pulled him toward the Relief Society room where the class was being held. Let Caleb and his retinue figure out where Sunday School was if they were going to stand around.

"Everyone seems nice," Elliot said.

"Yes," Paige said, sitting down in a huff. Elliot took a seat next to her. She almost turned around to check for Caleb but stopped herself. What did she care where he was? Becca's laugh signaled their arrival in the seats directly behind them.

Elliot reached over and took Paige's hand in his. "I think I like holding your hand," he said. He grinned at her with a soft look in his eyes.

She gaped at him. She'd only meant to pull him toward the class, but now she realized she'd given him the idea she wanted to hold his hand. There was nothing left to do but allow it. It wasn't a big deal, and she didn't want to make a big fuss. Heat crawled up her neck, as if someone stared at the back of her head. Caleb could probably see everything. Now she regretted being in such a hurry to get to class.

Throughout the next hour, Elliot's thumb caressed the skin on the back of her hand. It wasn't unpleasant. It'd been a while since she'd held a man's hand . . . but it wasn't Elliot's hand she wanted to hold.

Caleb and Becca whispered back and forth, though she couldn't really hear what they were saying. Why Becca? What did he see in a girl whose laugh sounded like a donkey and was as loud as a foghorn? Then again, it shouldn't surprise Paige if it came down to the holy trinity of marriageable qualities men looked for—young, pretty, and inexperienced. They looked for girls young enough to mold into their version of the perfect wife. They wanted a girl that hadn't been outside her parents' home long enough to develop bothersome qualities, like opinions.

Becca was far too young for Caleb. She was almost a full decade younger. That was only Paige's opinion, and Caleb certainly wouldn't care what Paige thought. Besides, he was a grown man. He could date whomever he wanted, even if he made a crappy choice. It made his snotty comments from the day before seem hypocritical, and that annoyed her. Her irritation with him increased.

"So how have the wedding plans been going?" Elliot whispered.

"About as well as you'd expect. Fun with a little dash of drama," she said, rolling her shoulders, trying to release the buildup of annoyance.

"Drama?"

"Alisa and Caleb are converts, and their parents weren't happy about it."

"Oh, yes, I can imagine that would be hard," Elliot said. He paused for a second or two before continuing. "Is Caleb the one that got away?"

Paige glanced at Elliot in shock. "Why do you ask?"

"He nearly fractured my hand when you introduced us. It then occurred to me he's both a Marine, and you used to know him."

"He nearly fractured your hand? What was he thinking?"

"Sending me a message?"

"About what? I haven't talked to him for almost ten years. And he's made it very clear this entire time he barely tolerates me."

Elliot smiled a sad smile and sighed. "I'm not sure I'm so confident in his indifference. If he were staying in Utah, I'd worry about the competition."

"That's a gigantic leap in logic, don't you think?"

"I may not be an expert in the human condition, but I understand other guys," Elliot said. "Seems awfully territorial for someone who is merely tolerating your presence."

"Really? Much like you when you grabbed me around the waist and practically smashed me against your side?"

"That bothered you?" Elliot asked, surprised.

"Well, if we're talking about males who feel the need to be territorial . . ." Paige said. "Seems you don't really have a place to talk."

"Paige, I meant nothing by it other than trying to be close to you—"

"I hoped to get through the wedding with as little drama as possible, for Alisa's sake. Every time I turn around, it seems I'm stepping in it. Between their parents, and now you—"

"I'm truly not trying to make your life harder," Elliot said. "I didn't think it would upset you like it has. You didn't seem to mind holding my hand, but I just wonder if there's more to the situation than you're willing to see."

"I think you're reading too much into it. Even if there was something there, like you insinuate, I won't need to worry about any secret crushes. He'll be out of the state by month's end, and it won't matter after that."

"The lady doth protest too much," Elliot said.

Paige pulled her hand out of Elliot's. "You're not funny."

"I wasn't trying to be," he said. Paige glared at him.

"I'll be right back," she said. She stood up and made her way to the door. She wandered down the hallway of the church. Her heart nearly galloped out of her chest, and she blinked back tears. How could Elliot be so cruel? Caleb felt nothing for her anymore, and to suggest it was hurtful. She was approaching the foyer when she heard voices.

"Look, it's not something we need to talk about right now," Tom said.

"How is 'how many children we plan on having' not important?"

"That's not what I'm saying," Tom said. "I'm saying why discuss this now? We have a wedding to get through. Your parents are not making that easy."

"You knew it wouldn't be easy before you came out here."

"Right, but I didn't think they'd be so toxic."

"Toxic? That's rich. Stop making my parents out to be yours," she said. "At least mine can talk to one another without starting World War III."

"This wedding is turning into a waste of time and money anyway," he said. "We should have just gotten married at the Savannah temple."

"What? So we exclude everyone we care about?"

"Yes, if it would have saved us the hassle of dealing with all this drama."

Paige slowly walked toward Alisa and Tom. Alisa looked like she was about to say something else when she saw Paige approaching them.

"Is Sunday School over?" Alisa asked, stepping away from her fiancé.

"Nearly. I needed a drink of water."

"Elliot looks like a friendly guy."

"He is," Paige answered.

"You haven't said much about him," Alisa said. "I didn't think you guys were that serious."

"We're not," Paige said. "Nothing has changed. I'm still trying to decide what's there, if anything. I've told him as much. We take it one date at a time."

Alisa nodded and glanced at Tom. He stood off to the side, watching them. The awkwardness hung thick in the air.

The bell rang, and the first wave of people left the building. Using the extra noise in the hallway, Paige leaned into Alisa.

"Are you going to be okay?" Paige asked.

"Yeah, I'm worried about Tom," Alisa said. "He's been a little touchy since we got here."

"I don't blame him for being gun shy about your parents," Paige said. "After what happened at the engagement party. And it's probably wedding jitters too. Marriage is a big step."

"I know that, Paige," Alisa said, biting her lip. "He's not the only one who's nervous. I wish he would be slightly more patient with my parents. I understand they haven't been very welcoming, but my parents just need time. His own parents' relationship is a horror show. He jumps to the worst possible conclusions about mine, as if they were his parents."

Paige hugged Alisa. "You've only got two more weeks, and then you'll be on your honeymoon. Then things can settle down."

A loud, grating laugh echoed down the hallway. Caleb and Becca walked into the foyer with Lucie in tow.

"That is so funny," Becca said.

"Everything all right?" Caleb asked.

"We're fine," Alisa said. "I'm taking a long Sunday nap when we get home. I think I'm getting a headache."

"Is there anything I can do?" Paige said, really getting worried for her friend. "Maybe the sleep will do you good."

Elliot walked up to Paige. "Can I talk to you a second?"

"Sure," she said, walking toward the bishops' offices. She made it a point not to look at Caleb.

"I wanted to say I'm sorry, Paige," Elliot said. "I swear my mouth runs off ahead of my brain sometimes."

"That's sweet, Elliot," Paige said. "I'm sorry too. I shouldn't be so sensitive. It's been a very long and weird week."

"If you ever need a break from the weird, call me," Elliot said. "We'll do something not wedding-ish."

"Thanks," she said, giving Elliot a squeeze. "I'll let you know."

She turned and her eyes immediately locked with Caleb's, as if he had been watching them talking. She gave him a slight smile but walked back to Alisa.

"We've been talking," Alisa said. "Caleb and the girls want to go do something, and I just want to go home. I'm not feeling well."

"If you didn't feel like going home right away, I guess you could come with us. I don't think any of us would care," Caleb said. "Give Tom your keys and he can drive Alisa home."

The thought of spending time watching Becca hang all over Caleb did not appeal to her. But it would mean a few precious minutes alone with him after dropping the Groves girls off. She almost said yes until she glanced over to where Elliot watched them. Paige's cheeks burned. There wasn't room for Elliot in the car. She couldn't accept an invitation to go somewhere without him from the man he suspected of being Paige's long-lost love. Paige and Elliot weren't exclusive necessarily, but it still didn't seem right.

"Thanks, Caleb. I should probably get your sister home if she's not feeling well," Paige said to him, examining his nearly expressionless face. Caleb's face was hard to read, but did she see disappointment there? She probably only saw it because she wanted to. "You guys go have fun."

Paige followed Tom and Alisa out of the church. She only looked back once, and saw Caleb also watching as Paige and the others walked toward her car. He led the two sisters to his car. What a disaster. A nap sounded amazing, as all she craved was being alone. She wouldn't have to put up with anyone suggesting certain people had feelings when they didn't. She wouldn't have to listen to the braying laughter of girls nearly a decade younger than men who had no business dating them. She wouldn't have to worry about her best friend and her best friend's fiancé. They were perfect for each other and the strife between them worried Paige.

Paige got in and started the engine while she waited for Tom and Alisa to get into the car. She watched from across the parking lot as Becca hung off Caleb's arm before reaching his car. He opened the door for her like a gentleman and made sure both girls got in. Paige turned her head before her stomach could clench anymore

Tom opened the door to the front seat for Alisa. "Didn't want to make you feel like a limo driver," he said, grinning, before getting in himself.

They drove the rest of the way back to Bountiful in silence. Paige dropped them off at the Watsons' and then went to her parents' house to crawl into her old bed.

She closed her eyes, feeling annoyed and depressed as she lay down. She hadn't counted on how hard being around Caleb this much would be. He was more handsome than ever, which added insult to injury. The injury because she couldn't fairly claim him as hers. That boat had sailed a long time ago, and by her choosing. The insult because nothing, even time, had lessened the amount of attraction she felt for him—and she had to watch as younger, prettier women threw themselves at him, and there was nothing she could rightfully do about it.

CHAPTER 10

Paige and Alisa stuffed envelopes with wedding invitations at the Watsons' kitchen table.

"Are you sure you still want to send these out? With a little over two weeks until the wedding, people may not receive them in time," Paige replied.

"Yes. I figure if they can't come, at least they knew it happened," Alisa said, licking another envelope and setting it aside.

"Excellent point. Plus, you might get more presents off your registry that way."

"One would hope," Alisa chuckled. "Tom and I have each lived on our own for so long we don't need much. That cherry red stand mixer would be nice, though."

The women giggled.

Caleb walked out from the hallway where the bedrooms were. Paige looked over at him as he wandered over to where the two friends sat. She looked back at the envelopes and sighed to herself. She hadn't talked to him since she'd seen him on Sunday, though she'd been over to the Watson house several times since then. What was there to talk about? His terrible taste in hang-out buddies? Or his insistence on only talking to her when it was absolutely necessary?

"Paige, I've been talking to Brent. He really wants to hang out before the wedding," he said. "I was wondering if you could take me to their house for a bit?"

"What about Alisa?" Paige asked. She refused to look at him. Looking at him meant being reminded how good-looking he was, or seeing him smirk crookedly, or staring at her with those amazing hazel eyes. All of it would make her stomach do flips in the absolutely most unfair way.

"Go. There's only a few left," Alisa said. "Tom should be back soon. But tell that dork Brent I don't forgive him for making you go there. I wanted to see Lindsay's boys too but there's just not enough time in the day for everything."

Paige gave her a small smile. "Only if you're sure. I never pass up a chance to hang out with my boys."

"Boys, as in two?" Caleb asked, looking from Alisa to Paige.

"Yes, there's Cameron and Will," Paige answered.

"Wow. I think the last I heard they were pregnant with Cameron."

"They are all boy. You'll like them," she said, grinning at Caleb.

Paige got her purse and keys. She looked back to make sure Caleb was behind her. He opened the door for her and followed her to the car. The thought of Caleb as a dad to his own boys made Paige feel a little swoony. She needed to knock that off. Even if he eventually was a dad to boys, or any kids for that matter, the likelihood of them being hers as well was slim. No point in getting excited for something wasn't going to happen.

They spent the rest of the drive in silence. Brent Groves. In high school, it had been the four of them—Alisa, Paige, Caleb and Brent. If it wasn't Brent and Caleb getting into minor trouble, then the four of them could be seen running around town together goofing off and having fun. It was still weird to think that Brent was now related to her. But if she had to choose a good guy for her sister, Brent would have been at the top of the list. Even if he was prone to being a dork, he was a good-hearted one. He'd graduated from high school, went on his mission, graduated from college and worked his hardest to make Paige's sister the happiest he could possibly make her.

They could hear Will crying loudly as they approached Lindsay and Brent's front door. Paige knocked and Brent answered.

"Caleb!" he said, giving the other man a bro hug. "Come in."

Paige looked around when she got through the door and found Lindsay in the TV room bouncing a crying Baby Will.

"He's got an ear infection," Lindsay explained. "I gave him some medicine a little while ago, but it doesn't seem to help."

"Do you want me to take him for a minute?"

"Yes, I have to find Cameron. He's been quiet for longer than five minutes."

"Um, yeah. Go find him."

She took the baby from her sister. The little boy's head was ablaze, and he whimpered in his aunt's arms. "Oh, honey, I'm sorry you feel icky. Shall we go for a walk and introduce you to your daddy's friend, Caleb?"

She drifted over to where the two men were chatting in the foyer.

"This is Will. He's not feeling very good. Ear infection."

"Hey, buddy," Caleb said, taking the baby's hand, pretending to shake it. Will tucked his head in his aunt's neck and gave a shuddering breath. "Yeah, he's warm. Even his hand is feverish."

"*RAWR*," a loud growl came from at the top of the stairs.

"And that is our dinosaur, Cameron," Brent said.

Cameron rushed Caleb.

"Oo, what a scary dinosaur," he said, laughing as Cameron ran into the TV room to continue his reign of terror.

"Come all the way in and have a seat," Brent suggested. "How've you been?"

"Good," Caleb replied. He glanced over at Paige as she bounced the baby. "I'm still stationed at the Marine Corps Air Station in Beaufort, South Carolina. I'm more into training than flying nowadays, but it's still great to get up in the air myself when I can."

"Yeah, I can imagine."

Cameron crawled onto the couch. Still growling, he climbed up onto the rear of the couch to growl at Will.

"How's your job treating you?" Caleb said, eyeing Cameron as he teetered on the edge of the furniture.

"Busy, always busy," Brent said, leaning back. "Hey, Cam, get off the couch like that. Your mom will have a fit."

Cameron jumped off the back of the couch to the ground behind it. He pounced on Paige's leg and pulled on Will's pajama leg. Paige shushed him, so Cameron ran away from her.

"We got some new building contracts. There are so many new buildings going up around the valley," Brent stated.

Cameron climbed up on Caleb's armchair and jumped off. "Hey, little man, be careful," Caleb said. "Yeah, we noticed all the construction coming in from the airport."

Cameron clambered over his dad and sat on the arm of the couch. "Dad, Dad, Dad, Dad," he said as he tapped Brent on the head. "Watch me."

The boy stood up, lost his balance, and before anyone could react, he fell backward, landing in a pile of toys on the floor. The room went silent for a fraction of a second before everyone reacted at once.

"Cameron!" Brent said, grabbing his son. Cameron sucked in a deep breath and screamed at the top of his lungs. A dozing Will immediately started wailing.

Lindsay raced down the stairs. "What happened?"

"Cameron fell off the couch," Paige answered.

Lindsay swept Cameron into her arms. "Baby, are you okay? Did you fall?"

Cameron could only answer her with hiccupping sobs. He snuggled into his mother. By the time Paige had calmed Will down, Cameron seemed to have recovered himself. She strolled over to where her sister and nephew stood snuggling.

“Hi, Mr. Dinosaur,” Paige said, rubbing her finger up and down his arm. “You feel better now?”

He peeked out over to her, big tears running down his face. “Paige, I fell.”

“I know,” she said. “I saw. Probably shouldn’t do that again, huh?”

He tucked his head into his mother’s neck. “Mom?” his voice muffled. “Can I have a popsicle?”

Paige struggled to cover her laugh with the back of her hand. She peeked over at Brent and Caleb. They both had amused smiles on their faces.

“Sure, baby,” Lindsay said, walking him over to the refrigerator. “What flavor did you want?”

“Blue,” he answered.

Lindsay put him down and got his ice pop out. She handed it to him, and he made his way slowly over to where his toys were.

“Ugh, I’m so glad boys are made of whatever it is they’re made of,” Lindsay said, taking Will back from Paige. “I’m not sure I’m going to survive another thirteen years or more of stuff like this. Honey, if we have any more kids, I insist the next one be a girl.”

Brent and Paige laughed.

“So, does that mean I get to buy the shotgun I want, if it is a girl?” Brent asked.

“No,” Lindsay said, sitting down beside her husband.

“It’s practically a requirement for a father of a daughter to own one,” Caleb responded. “Don’t worry, Brent, I’ll hook you up.”

“Caleb, do not encourage him,” Lindsay said, glaring at him.

Caleb sat down on the ground near to where Cameron ate his popsicle. He pushed a firetruck toward him. Cameron just watched it. He hugged the arm without the popsicle to his chest but didn't reach out for the toy.

"So, Caleb," Brent said. "Do you think you might have to do any more tours in the Middle East?"

"There's always that possibility," he said, driving the firetruck around for Cameron to watch. "I haven't been called up in a while. I expect that's mostly because I'm training, but that never stopped them from sending guys out."

"Here's hoping you don't for a long time," Brent replied. "Oh, before I forget. I wanted to congratulate you and Alisa on your baptism. I think that's fantastic."

"Thanks. It's been a long time in coming," Caleb said, peeking at Paige. Paige had to keep her mouth from falling open but walked away instead. A long time in coming? The accusatory look he'd given her graduation night would have said otherwise.

Caleb tried once more to hand the firetruck to Cameron. The boy had the popsicle fully entrenched in his mouth and his other arm snuggled against his chest. Cameron shook his head.

"Hey, buddy, can I see your arm?" Caleb asked. He reached out and inspected the limb. Caleb gently touched a red spot and Cameron whimpered. "I think he hurt his arm. Look." The arm appeared slightly red and swollen.

Lindsay handed the baby back to Paige and knelt down to inspect her son.

"Cameron, does your arm hurt, baby?" The little boy nodded. Lindsay looked up to her husband. "What do you think we should do? I don't want to take the chance that it's broken. Though how he could have broken anything just falling off the couch, I don't know."

"He fell on top of all those toys," Paige said.

"Whatever you want to do, Lindsay," Brent said, kneeling down next to his son.

"I'd feel better if we'd at least take him to an urgent care or something," Lindsay replied. "If it's not broken, just bruised, then at least we'd know."

"Okay, then let's do that. You take Cameron to the van," he responded. "I'll grab the keys. Can you guys stay here with Will?"

"Of course," Paige replied.

The parents rushed their little boy out of the house. Paige looked over at Caleb. "Poor Cameron, I hope he'll be okay," Paige said. "Mr. Will, I know you don't feel good. Let's get you back to sleep."

"Can I try?" Caleb said, coming up to her and holding his arms out.

"Sure, thank you," she answered. She handed Will over. "He gets heavy after a while."

She was sure Will would start screaming and reach out to her, but he snuggled his head against Caleb's chest and quieted.

"Traitor," she said to the baby, smiling.

"Babies like me," Caleb responded.

"I can see that. Or maybe it's because you're a soldier and soldiers are helpful," Paige said.

Caleb grinned at her. "You mean officers are helpful."

"Yes, sorry—officers," she said.

"Big officers," he said, rubbing Will's back.

"No, that's Big Caleb," Paige said, trying to smother her giggles behind her hand.

"Well, if you insist." His beautifully crooked grin spread across his face.

He walked Will around the room, bouncing him a little. What was it about holding babies that made guys, and in this case, Caleb, look hotter? She had to shake herself out of the trance she found herself in while watching the sweet sight. Even she could admit that to herself.

"I'll get a washcloth to cool that head off," Paige said, going into the kitchen. When she came back, Caleb sat in the armchair with Will snuggling in. "Is he okay? Are you?"

"I'm fine," Caleb said, giving Paige a slight smile. "He's still warm though."

Paige lay the cloth on the baby's head and sat down on the couch near them. As she watched Caleb snuggle with the baby, her heart skipped a beat. Once upon a time, that might have been their child he held so tenderly. He rocked the chair slowly back and forth. They sat in silence for a while, waiting for Will to fall asleep. Will's eyes drooped and then closed.

"Is he asleep?" Caleb asked.

Paige nodded.

"Is it weird I'm holding the baby of the guy who was my best friend in high school?" Caleb asked.

"Not any weirder than the fact that you're holding my younger sister's baby," Paige replied. "I still can't wrap my head around the idea they're married to each other sometimes."

Caleb chuckled. "True. How did that even happen?"

"Well, the timing was just right," she said. "He'd gotten off his mission about a year after she graduated from high school. They were in the singles' ward together for a little while, and they clicked. I would have never looked at them when we were in high school and said, 'They're going to get married someday.' I guess they needed time to grow up."

Caleb nodded. "He seems really happy."

"I know my sister is," Paige added. "Brent's given her everything she's ever wanted—a wonderful home with an honorable priesthood holder, two beautiful babies so far, and a nice house where they can raise those babies."

Caleb sat silently for a moment. "Are those things you want, too, still?"

She looked him in the eyes. "I haven't changed my mind about the things I want. I haven't found someone I want them with. Lindsay would say I'm too picky—that I won't give nice men enough of a chance. I keep trying to tell her forever is a long time to be with someone I only like."

Caleb grinned. "I understand about the picky part. Lise says the same thing about me. I don't have a list per se of what I'm looking for. I figure that when I meet her, I'll have a powerful reaction. And since I joined the Marines, no one has made me feel that way."

For a moment, they stared at each other. The statement held so much unsaid that Paige found she couldn't sit still. She stood up and fled into the kitchen. The sudden urge to clean made it impossible for her to sit there and watch Caleb with her nephew. By the time she'd finished doing the dishes, swept the floor and scrubbed the counters, there was nothing left to do but pace the room. Why was she suddenly unable to take deep breaths? The things she needed to express to him crowded together in her throat, slowly choking her. The perfect moment to say what she needed to was here, but her heart beat like it wanted to pop out of her chest. She struggled to summon the courage. Every time she thought she had enough nerve, a sinking feeling hit her stomach, and the nerve deflated. She glanced over at him. He sat there in the armchair watching her.

"What's up?" he asked. "You pace like that when you are thinking too hard."

She bit her lip. He remembered.

"Caleb, I . . ." she said, breathing out. "I need to tell you something, but I've never found the right time. At Leatherby's, I wanted to after Tom said something, but well, that didn't work out. But it's important for me to say it. I really regret—"

Will stirred on Caleb's chest. His mewling cry got stronger the more awake he was. Caleb stood up and started walking him around.

Paige sighed. She took the cloth off the baby's head and wet it again before she put it back on.

"Let me take a turn," Paige said. Caleb handed Will to her. Will drifted off to sleep once more after Paige bounced and sang to him for a while. Caleb had leaned against the couch, continuing to watch her. She was just delaying and no closer to saying what she needed.

"What were you trying to say?" Caleb asked after a while. "You said you regretted something."

She glanced at him and sighed. "I don't expect anything from you, like a reaction, or for you to feel a certain way. I've thought about what to say a million times and it never comes out the way I want it to."

"Paige, you're rambling," Caleb said, but not unkindly. "What do you need to say?"

The interruption slowed her momentum, and her stomach sank once more. Her brain cycled through feelings so fast she couldn't keep up with it all. Tears swam in her eyes. She glanced over at Caleb. Instead of bored or impatient, he looked concerned.

"Is Will asleep again?" Paige asked, taking deep breaths, trying to get herself under control. Caleb nodded.

"I'm taking Will upstairs and see if I can get him to go down in his bed," she said, rushing up the stairs. Once through the door to Will's room, Paige took a really deep breath to keep the tears pooling in her eyes from falling. *Nice one, Paige,* she thought. *I can't even get through one sentence without practically bursting into tears. How am I supposed to get through everything else?*

She approached Will's crib and carefully laid him down. He stirred a little but settled down when she lightly rubbed his tummy. Paige continued the song she had been singing for him, using the time to convince her heart rate to slow down. She gently waved the cloth in the air to cool it down and placed it on his warm head again. Paige wiped moisture from the corners of her eyes. She had panicked and run away. She had to do something, say something. She didn't know if she'd get another chance with the wedding speedily coming. She pushed herself back upright and quietly closed the door. She took one more deep breath before heading down to the first floor.

Caleb hadn't moved from the spot where she'd left him. He looked up at her, and his beautiful hazel eyes pierced her to her soul. She had to hold herself back from irrationally running up and hugging him, wanting to be in his arms.

"Did he go down okay?" he asked.

"Yes," she said, hating that her voice sounded so unsteady. "Caleb, I—"

"Paige, if it's that hard to say, then don't say it."

"Will you give me a minute?" she snapped, tucking some hair behind her ear. "This is hard for me, but I have to say it because if I don't . . . If I don't, I don't want to have to wait another decade for you to stop hating me."

"Paige, I don't hate you."

"Sure. You've so clearly made that understood since you walked off the plane," Paige said angrily. She stopped herself before her temper got the better of her.

"I'm sorry," she said, putting her hand to her head. "All I'm trying to say is I know I deserve your anger. Graduation night, I let you walk away hurt and angry. I chickened out because I couldn't stand that look in your eyes. It was like someone was stabbing me in my gut. My parents weren't wrong, but I didn't know how to say it right, and it hurt you. I've felt so guilty because of that night and wished I could have talked to you before you left." Tears threatened to fall again. "It was the worst night of my life. I've wished so many times things could have turned out differently, that I could have said something else, something that would have helped you understand. And I know that I can't do or say anything now that would make it better, but I didn't want you to think I—"

The garage door's motor hummed as it opened, signaling Brent and Lindsay were home. Her momentum gone, there was no way to get it back. She stood in front of Caleb, her chest heaving with her struggle to keep from collapsing into a mess of tears. He stood there staring at her, stunned. Was he angry, or confused? Or smug? Why wasn't he saying anything? Her self-control cracked the longer he stayed silent. When she heard Lindsay's voice right behind the door, it all became too much. Paige escaped back up the stairs because she couldn't face her sister or Brent in the state she was in.

She flew into the bathroom and locked the door. Leaning against the wall, she took several deep breaths before she blew out the air shakily. She snatched up some facial tissue so she could drain away the moisture. She needed to look a little more composed before she went back downstairs. When she settled down enough, she rejoined everyone in the TV room. Cameron was showing Caleb his purple cast.

"Paige, look," he said, running up to her.

"Wow, that is a great color," she declared. "Lindsay, do you have a pen somewhere? Cam, can I sign your cast?"

Lindsay got a permanent marker, and Paige put her name on the cast.

"Caleb," Cameron said. "Sign it?"

Caleb knelt down next to the boy and took the pen from Paige. He signed his name next to hers on the cast.

"Thank you, guys, so much for watching the baby," Lindsay said. "Made things so much easier and quicker without him fussing the entire time."

"He's upstairs asleep now," Paige replied.

"Thank you," Lindsay said, relieved. "I'm going to take Cameron upstairs and put him to bed as well. Caleb, don't feel you have to rush off. Stay for a bit."

Brent and Caleb sat back down in the TV room. Paige's insides vibrated with nervous energy. She began picking up the toys Cameron had left all over.

"Paige, sit down," Brent said. "You're not here to clean up after Cam."

She slowly sat down on the couch with Brent. She couldn't help glancing at Caleb as she did and noticed he looked back at her. His intent stare drove her insane because nothing could be read there.

"So, two boys now, huh?" Caleb said to Brent.

"Yeah, they're great," Brent replied. "When are you getting around to having your own? Or are the Marines keeping you too busy?"

"Have to have a wife first," Caleb answered. "Then I'll think about the kids part."

"You know what Brigham Young said about single men over the age of thirty," Brent said smiling. "You don't have too many years before you're considered a menace."

Paige couldn't help grinning at that one. An amused smirk spread across Caleb's face.

"I figure Brother Brigham will cut me a little slack since I've only been a member for a few years," Caleb replied. "I want to make sure the woman I marry is pretty special. Then having those kids won't be an *if,* but a *when*. You'd be surprised how hard it is to find a girl who wants marriage, a career, kids, *and* can put up with the Marines."

Brent nodded sagely. "I hear you. That's how I felt about finding someone that wanted the same things I did. Lindsay and I wanted the same things. It was really cool actually because it was almost like she'd reached into my head and planned it out the way I saw it. So, when we met, we just knew what we had to do to make the plan happen. She's been amazingly supportive while I finished school, and we worked together. I couldn't have asked for a better partner."

"Are you talking me up?" Lindsay said, sitting down between Paige and Brent. She leaned into his arm.

"Of course," he stated. "I can't give up a chance to brag about my wife."

Caleb glanced over at Paige and smiled. She returned it. It was nice to hear her sister and best friend from high school so happy together.

"Good," she laughed. "Caleb, it's been forever. I'm sorry we had such a crazy night. I'm so excited for Alisa. Tell me about this Tom guy."

Caleb told Lindsay about how he met Tom and his help in the twins' conversion. It was fascinating hearing about it from Caleb's perspective. He felt the Spirit strongly when he was investigating. When it came time to commit, it wasn't a hard decision for him to make. His strong faith was attractive, but it was more than that. Her admiration for him went beyond physical attraction. He'd always been passionate about things he cared about when she had known him before. Now that passion was for more important matters, like his career and his relationship with his Heavenly Father. How would it be if his more grown-up passion also included a piece for her too?

"That is so amazing," Lindsay replied. "And you're still not married. It's surprising some girl in South Carolina hasn't snapped you up yet."

"Um," Caleb said, looking distinctly more uncomfortable as he glanced at Paige.

"You're probably super picky like Paige is," Lindsay said, laughing.

"Hon, I seriously doubt it's for lack of those girls trying," Brent suggested. "Knowing Caleb."

"Wow, I didn't realize how late it was," Paige said, standing up. "I should probably get Caleb back to his parents' house."

"Hey, let's not go this long again before talking," Brent replied. "Maybe do some guy stuff next time?"

"It may be a while, but I'll look forward to it," Caleb said, standing himself to follow Paige outside.

Caleb and Paige walked in silence to the car. They were quiet as they drove back to the Watsons'. Paige's brain burned with curiosity. She wanted to know what he was thinking, but she couldn't bring herself to start another potentially awkward conversation. She pulled up to the curb, however Caleb didn't get out right away.

"You're not coming in?" he asked.

She searched his face. "No, I don't really have a reason to," she said, her feelings and her common sense warring with each other. *Give me a reason, Caleb,* she thought to herself. *Tell me you forgive me at least.*

"We'll see you tomorrow?"

"Probably."

"I'll see you then. Thanks again for taking me over to see Brent. It was nice to see him and meet his kids—your nephews. Gosh, that's weird." He shook his head.

Paige gave him a small smile. "I know."

He got out and waved at her as she put the car into drive and drove away. She looked in the rearview mirror. He stood on the sidewalk, watching her drive away. She was too far gone to deny it, and everyone around her had been right. Her feelings for Caleb had not really changed over the years, just the level of hope she held that things could be different. She was still completely in love with him.

Holding Elliot's hand yesterday made her realize something she hadn't wanted to admit to herself. It wasn't just Elliot who had failed to inspire admiration and romantic feelings in her. Any other man she'd dated hadn't either. And it came down to the fact that they weren't Caleb. She measured every man she dated against the sweet relationship Caleb and she had shared. None of them had come even close to being the same.

Unfortunately, tonight had clarified a lot for Paige. She had done what she had set out to do. She apologized to Caleb like she had wanted for years. But like he'd done a decade ago, he'd disappointed her by leaving her pleas unacknowledged. Caleb had made it obvious any remaining feelings were all on her side. No one could be forced to forgive, so she could only draw comfort that at least she'd had the chance to ask for it. The ball was in his court, and it looked like he had decided to take it home with him instead of playing.

Chapter 11

Alisa sat in the middle of the room on a chair at the Ellis house, her hair and clothes covered in bows and ribbon. For a last-minute bridal shower, quite a few of Paige and Alisa's old high school friends had shown up. Lindsay had come too, though she'd had to bring Becca and Lucie with her. Karen and Liz sat next to each other in a tense silence on the edge of the room.

Alisa pulled the tissue out of the next bag and held up a very see-through negligee with a matching robe. All the women oh'd and ah'd, and Becca and Lucie let out little cat calls.

Alisa laughed, and her cheeks turned a few colors of pink. "Who bought me the lingerie?"

"Guilty," Paige said. "And I got the biggest bow I could find."

"I'm putting this at the bottom of a bag. Tom will love this, but he'll be downright obnoxious with jokes about me in it."

They all chuckled. Paige pulled the bow off the gift bag and stuck it to the back of Alisa's head.

Lindsay stood up and handed Alisa her present. Alisa tore open the package to find a his-and-hers bath bomb and bath oil set.

"Thank you, Lindsay," Alisa said. "I'm going to love this."

"Now you have to find a bathtub big enough for the both of you," Lindsay said.

"Who said I was sharing?"

"I'll say nothing," Lindsay said, grinning. "I wasn't sure you'd want to go around smelling like sandalwood and musk."

"Anything to take a nice, long, hot bath. And thank you for not having a bow or ribbon on your present. This game is so ridiculous."

"I don't think Tom will complain when we explain the rules," Paige said.

As if magically summoned, there came a knock at the door. Paige opened it and found Tom and Caleb standing there. "There's not too much more manly stuff we can do to keep ourselves distracted, short of finding a firing range nearby," Tom said. Then he noticed Alisa. "What happened to you?"

"Come with me, Tom," Paige said as she escorted Tom over to his fiancé. "The rules are she cannot take any of the ribbons or bows off until you give her a kiss. For every kiss, she gets to take one off."

A wide grin spread across his face. "I think I like this game."

Paige stood to the side while Tom kissed Alisa repeatedly. Caleb stood next to her. "Where did you get the idea for this game?"

"This is a generational tradition of Ellis bridal showers," Paige said.

"Has my mom been behaving?" he murmured, so only Paige could hear.

"Yes, she hasn't talked much, but she's still taking part in the shower."

He nodded.

Paige laughed when Tom tried to take apart a bow, claiming they were individual ribbons. "Oh, Tom, stop cheating."

"Hey, is this all for you?" he said, looking through the bags. "Oo, what's this?"

He pulled out the negligee. Alisa groaned. "I knew I should have hidden it better."

He put it up to his own body. "Honey, I think they got the wrong size."

Alisa kissed Tom and pulled the lingerie out of his hands. "This is for two weeks from now."

Paige and Liz handed out the light luncheon. For a while Paige moved around the room and talked to each of the ladies who supported Alisa. Every once in a while, she glanced over at Caleb. Most of the time he stood back and talked to Tom. Their eyes locked once, and she had to ask the woman talking to her to repeat herself. She sighed. It was a little unfair that even after ten years he could still distract her like that. When they were in school, even her parents could tell what classes they had together because her grades would be slightly lower than all the rest of them. Back then, he had been a fun and funny kind of distraction. He lived to make her laugh. But that was before graduation night.

The party wound down, and Liz, Paige, and Alisa started cleaning up. The men pitched in as well. Caleb offered to wash dishes. After he'd been at the sink for a few minutes, Paige approached him with a dish towel in hand. She grabbed the glass punch bowl and dried it.

"I can do that too," Caleb said.

"Eh. Many hands make light work," she said, reaching up and putting the bowl away. She grunted a little as she reached up on her tiptoes to put it in the cabinet. When she turned, she caught him watching her.

He cleared his throat. "I know it's none of my business, but I wondered about that Elliot guy."

Paige smirked. "I'm sure you would."

Caleb gave her a look. "I'm curious about what kind of guy he is."

"He's our age. He moved to Utah from Boston so he could work toward a partnership in a law firm here in Salt Lake. We're dating, but beyond that I couldn't tell you. It's just one date at a time."

Caleb nodded. "A lawyer, huh?"

Paige shrugged. "Yes. What about it?"

"It'd be nice to have a six-figure income at your disposal, eventually."

Paige glared at Caleb. "Did you seriously just say that? I know we haven't talked in a long time, but I didn't think you'd think me capable of that. I don't need a man to support me. Otherwise, I would have gotten married a long time ago."

"Fair enough. You're so different from the girl I knew in high school."

"In a good way or a bad way?"

"I'm not sure yet."

Paige stared at him, then clenched her jaw. Really? He was going to insult her to her face in her parents' house? She threw her cloth down on the counter and turned to leave the kitchen.

"Paige," he said. "Come back. That came out wrong. I meant who you are now is a surprise to me. You're less shy, more confident."

Paige turned around and eyed him suspiciously. She grabbed another serving dish, dried it off, and put it away. "Thanks."

"Elliot seems to be a nice guy."

"He is."

"But?" Caleb asked.

"That's it," she said. "He's a nice guy."

"No butterflies, no heart palpitations?"

Paige chuckled. "It doesn't always work that way, you know. I may decide I like him too much to let him get away. Maybe some other guy will come along, and I'll feel the same for him as I did . . . Well, anyway, I'm living my life and trusting that Heavenly Father knows what's best for me. And if that's Elliot, then maybe I'll start to notice the butterflies and palpitations."

Caleb examined her face. "I doubt it. You don't go for the blond beanpole type."

"I seem to recall I went for the dark-haired beanpole type once. Is hair color really that important?"

"So, you're into the friendly and passively laid-back doormats?"

"As opposed to blunt and patronizing leathernecks?"

He shook his head. "Blunt, yes. Patronizing?"

"Irritating."

"I just call it like I see it."

"At least with Elliot, I'd stay in one place for longer than two years." The minute it popped out of her mouth, she regretted it.

He looked at her impassively for a minute, closed the dishwasher and leaned against the counter. "Marine life isn't for everyone—I'll give you that. They haven't moved me for a while. Probably because Tom and Alisa were meant to get together. It can get old constantly having to pack everything up, move to a new place, try to get used to a new area and find friends. But sometimes it's more like an adventure than a burden. It's all about perspective."

"I think Lise saw it like you do—one big adventure," Paige said. "And now she'll be taking it with Tom."

"What about you? You almost signed up for that life. Would you have seen moving around as some big adventure?"

"Not necessarily—but then again, it wasn't too bad when I was on my mission. We did a lot of moving around with transfers. But right after high school, maybe it would have been harder for me. I didn't have my education yet, so I wouldn't have had a job to keep me busy. Now it wouldn't be too bad because teachers are needed everywhere. It's just that if I wanted to do something other than teach some day, it might be hard to do without setting down roots somewhere."

"So, this Elliot guy is your best bet for that."

"Elliot is nearly last on the list of what to consider when I decide what I want out of life. I'm perfectly happy as I am right now."

"I don't know, Paige," he said, folding his arms. "You always thought you were the smartest person in the room—not that you were wrong most of the time. But you used to exaggerate as a form of bluffing. I have a feeling that hasn't changed much over the years, considering you're trying to sell to me how content you are."

"Rest assured, Caleb," Paige said. "I haven't been languishing away in Utah the last decade. I've been too busy with college, a mission, and my career."

"Time spent wisely, no one can argue about that," he said, giving her an impish look. "I would hate to think you'd spend hours and hours staring at pictures of me in our yearbook."

Paige rolled her eyes.

"Caleb," Karen said, coming up to them. "Would you help me get these gifts to the house?"

Karen looked at Paige. "Thank you for throwing Alisa a bridal shower. Amongst all the other things we've needed to do, this was one thing I forgot about. But I suppose you had a better network of friends."

Liz came into the kitchen. It was feeling crowded. "Oh, someone did the dishes."

"Thank Caleb," Paige said.

"Thank you, Caleb," Liz said, giving Caleb a sad smile.

"My pleasure, Sister Ellis," he said.

Liz walked out the kitchen mumbling, "Never thought I'd hear the day."

Caleb grinned at Paige. Paige couldn't help giggling.

"Mom, Tom and I will get all this stuff," he said, taking the bags from his mother.

After Caleb left, Karen turned back to Paige. "You know, for all that your church teaches about families, I never could get over the fact that it does a marvelous job of tearing them apart."

"Mrs. Watson, it goes both ways. Some families in our church have children who stop practicing, and the way they live their lives makes it hard for those families to accept. It's a struggle to find the right balance of tolerance and supportive love, whether you're a member of our church or not."

"But excluding family based solely on their membership is the thing I find the hardest to accept."

"It's only because the temple is our most sacred place. You're invited literally anywhere else in our church—except there. Not even every member can go there. I don't think I can say anything that will help you feel better about any of it. Not unless we sit down and have a very long missionary discussion about temples and forever families. I know you don't want that. Alisa wishes you'd be happy about gaining another son into the family."

"Why? So, I could feel better about having a potential daughter-in-law that's Mormon too? We've already had this discussion with them several times, and I really don't want to get into it again, least of all with you."

Paige sighed. She was trying her hardest to keep her temper under control. That was one thing Paige and Karen had in common. She couldn't imagine having to be her daughter-in-law with the way they were and have to listen to her needle the Church all the time.

"Accept it or not," Paige said, pushing past Karen. "The only thing I'm interested in is making sure Lise's wedding is the happiest day of her life. I'm sure she hopes the same thing from you. We don't have to be members of the same church to do that."

Chapter 12

Paige, Alisa and Karen sat around the Watsons' kitchen table. Alisa had her three-ring wedding binder open.

"I called the florist, and they'll have the topiaries to the reception center by late morning the day before," Alisa said. "That way we can have them set up the ring ceremony. What's the status of the cake tasting, Mom?"

"We're going tomorrow morning. And then we'll be running over to Phillipe's and getting your last fitting," Karen said.

"Wow, this is getting so real," Alisa exclaimed.

"I know. I'm so excited for you," Paige said "Mrs. Watson, will you and Mr. Watson be on the temple grounds when they come out?"

Karen stiffened. "We will. Like beggars waiting for our handouts."

"Mom," Alisa begged. "Please? You'll be the first person I want to see."

"I'm not interested in discussing this anymore, Alisa Anne," Karen said, standing up from the table.

Alisa sighed as her mother left the room. Paige rubbed her friend's back.

The front door opened, and Tom and Caleb walked through. Tom came over to Alisa and kissed her. Alisa clung to his neck for a moment before allowing him to sit down.

"Need help with anything?" Tom asked.

Alisa took in a shuddering breath. "I think we've got the fort held down so far. Just a few odds and ends to take care of tomorrow, and we'll be set," Alisa said.

"Finally," Tom said, running his hands down his face. "I can't wait until this is over, and we go on our honeymoon."

"Have your mom or dad called?" Alisa asked.

"My mom is coming. She's flying in the day before. I haven't heard from my dad yet."

Alisa's face pinched, and a grimaced spread across it. "What is his problem? It's not like we're asking him to shut himself in a room with her alone the whole time."

"She puts him on edge is all," Tom said.

"You'd think as grownups they could put aside their differences for one day for the sake of their only son."

"You've only seen the tiniest bit of it," Tom said defensively. "Things were rough until they got divorced. It's better when they aren't in close proximity."

"I didn't say they had to make up and be best friends," Alisa retorted. "Couldn't they attempt to at least ignore each other for one day?"

"I wouldn't talk about parents being on their best behavior," Tom said. "Because I got such a warm welcome when I got here."

Paige slowly stood up from the table. She locked eyes with Caleb, and they both made their way outside to the patio. Paige sat down on the Watsons' old wooden porch swing. Caleb sat next to her. He swung them back and forth. It was something they had done a lot back when they were together. She glanced at the picture window to check on the arguing couple, but the sunlight reflected off the glass making seeing through it impossible. It put Caleb in her line of sight, and she examined him as he lazily pushed the old swing.

Paige's brain was going a million miles an hour. She was at war with herself. She enjoyed being close to Caleb when they could sit near each other without being argumentative. For the moment, there seemed to be a nice, relaxed ease between them, and she couldn't help but miss that. Yet, she waited for the moment when one of them would react to the other, and then the gauntlet would fall again. That happened all too commonly this week.

Paige hated it. She didn't want to argue with him. There was something about him that made her extra sensitive to what he said and did. He seemed to welcome every chance he got to push her buttons. It was disheartening and exhausting. She'd rather get along with him and wished he would treat her closer to how he did in high school. He loved to make her laugh, and even if she was in a snit, she'd be laughing before too long. He never took her temper seriously. Times had changed, and they'd grown. He didn't have to put up with her temper, and maybe this was his way of showing her so. She hoped that despite everything, he would leave in a couple of weeks with nothing existing between them but a cordial, mutual well-wishing. If she wanted it, it would be up to her to take the higher road, as hard as that was sometimes.

She was hyper-aware of how close they sat together on the seat. Their shoulders lightly touched every time he pushed back as they swung back and forth. The heat from his body radiated through his t-shirt onto the skin of her shoulder. Warmth traveled up her arm and into her belly. It didn't help that she sat right in his cologne's halo. It was woodsy and musky and a perfect complement to his natural smell.

She glanced over at him.

"Do you think they'll be okay?" Paige asked.

Caleb shrugged. "Tom's had it hard. I don't blame him with how my parents have been. I wish I could make this easier for him."

"I hope he's not having doubts now. That would break Lise's heart."

"That's not it at all," Caleb said, searching her eyes with his gorgeous hazel ones. Paige's heart fluttered. "Tom is head over heels for Lise. It took him almost a month after he met her to get the courage to ask me if he could date her."

Paige gave Caleb a grin. "He asked you? That's so cute."

"He didn't want any weirdness between us. Tom's a great guy, and I saw he'd be great for her. She didn't make it easy for him, though. She turned him down a couple of times before she said she'd go out with him."

Paige chuckled. "That sounds like her, but this went fast. Seems like one day she was telling me she's dating this great guy. Then, the next, she's calling me, telling me they're engaged. She surprised me how quickly she decided to marry him. She's usually so cautious about such big decisions."

"It didn't take Tom very long to know he wanted to marry her," Caleb said, with a wistful smile.

"That's why their fighting worries me," she said, turning her torso a bit to try and get a peek into the picture window. The move snuggled her right up against him with her bent leg resting against his. His face looked as worried as she felt. "Getting married is stressful enough without all this fighting."

"He's done pretty well considering," Caleb said, leaning his arm along the back of the swing. "You haven't been around to see the crap my mom and dad have been putting him through. They use him as target practice every chance they get. I've tried talking to them about backing off, but they're not listening. If I had known it would be this hard, I would have made other arrangements for him."

"But it seems as the wedding gets closer, the less obliging he is. Not that I blame him at all. He's doing better than I would have," Paige replied. She looked down to hide her smile. Caleb, or maybe Alisa, would know better than anyone.

"I wish I could make my parents see how much this hurts all of us. I can't understand why it matters so much to them what religion we practice. They've never been very religious, so you wouldn't think they'd care. It took me by surprise they were so against it. Alisa shared my certainty, so we thought they'd see this wasn't some fanciful notion of ours. Why does it have to cause such contention when it's so wonderful?"

"It's not the gospel that causes the contention," she said, reaching out and laying her hand on his as it rested on his leg. "Feeling so very strongly about what you believe makes people uncomfortable. They get the impression you think yourself better than them because you're certain about something that might contradict what they believe. Sadly, that's not the point. We don't need to all believe the same things in order to get along."

"I always knew you were a smarty pants," he said, smiling at her and squeezing her hand. The smile actually reached his eyes and lit up his face. She felt lost in the warmth of his closeness and his smile for a moment until she realized how really close she was.

"That's what an eighteen-month mission will do for you," she said, blushing a little and looking away. She pulled her hand away gently and weaved her fingers together. "You see how the gospel changes people's lives. But you also see the fallout from those changes because others can't and won't understand."

"I always wondered how different my life would've been if I'd been more willing to listen in high school," he mumbled, like he was speaking to himself.

Blood rushed into Paige's cheeks even more and her pulse quickened. How many times had she wondered the same thing? To hear him say it out loud was exhilarating and painful.

"I guess you had to be ready to for it," she said. "Things were so . . . confusing back then. Maybe to be ready, you needed Tom."

He sighed. "I guess. The one thing I do know—being out in the Middle East changed me. I felt my mortality like I'd never experienced before. It's why when Tom started talking to me about what he believed, I was ready to listen. My parents never had a definitive answer about where we go after we die or what the purpose of all of this craziness is. But flying through the air dodging anti-aircraft fire, you realize merely existing isn't enough of an answer. Then things I'd heard you and your parents talking about, like eternal families and a loving Heavenly Father, made a lot more sense. I guess I was too young to appreciate why that would be important."

"It's so strange. I never really hoped that you would join the Church. You never took anything too seriously. It was one thing I liked about you, but it can have its drawbacks too."

"That kid no longer exists," he said, looking deep into her eyes.

No doubt about that, she thought.

"Do I seem so much different from what I was?" he asked.

"Yes, much different physically. But your personality . . . you turned out like I hoped you would—a little more serious and responsible but still kept your sense of humor."

"You wondered what I'd be like?"

Paige smiled despite herself. "I couldn't help it. You were an important part of my life once upon a time. And being your sister's best friend, it was hard not to pick up things about you every once in a while on social media."

Caleb gave her a soft smile. "Not that I stalked you online or anything, but I was curious too," he admitted. "And it's really hard to avoid the curiosity when it seemed like Lise had something to post about what you two were talking about every week. She loves you so much. So, I guess I was wrong the other day—I shouldn't have wondered what kind of person you'd turned out to be."

"And what kind of person did I turn out to be?" Paige challenged.

"Um, independent, professional, but still a know-it-all."

"You wouldn't want me to change who I am completely, would you?"

He searched her face a moment before answering. Had he leaned in closer? "No, definitely not. The only thing that astonishes me is that you're not married yet."

Now that was surprising. She'd already told him she'd thought that same thing about him, but she assumed he didn't really care if she was or not. "Forever never sounded appealing with any of the other men I dated."

"There's still Elliot. He seems eager enough."

"Elliot. We've barely started dating. He's nice enough, but it's complicated."

"No, it's not. You like him but not enough to marry him. You keep him just close enough so you don't feel lonely but not any closer so you don't give him the wrong idea."

"And you've spent one whole Sunday around us and that's what you've come up with?"

"Am I right?"

“That’s unfair, Caleb. We’ve only dated a little over a month, and I still don’t know how I feel about him.”

He shook his head. “If it was genuine love, you wouldn’t have to think about it so hard.”

“You’re still not married. What do you know about genuine love?”

“I used to know quite a bit about it, actually.” His voice lowered into a deeper, more vibrant register. “I’m not willing to settle. I’m just like you. I want all of it—the temple marriage, being together forever, raising a family in the gospel. All of it. But you can’t have that if you don’t have the right person first.”

His hazel eyes gazed into hers, meaning churning behind them. They mesmerized her, and she couldn’t look away. Her heart skipped beats as she struggled to draw in a breath to say something.

“Caleb, I . . .”

Paige's breath halted as his face moved in to close the small distance between them. Her entire body flushed with a warmth she’d long forgotten, her heart fluttering at his closeness. His lips feathered hers for one dizzying moment. Just as their lips met, the patio door flew open. They jumped, and Paige looked away, knowing her cheeks were crimson.

“Caleb, Becca and Lucie have been blowing up your cell phone for the past fifteen minutes. I hope you don’t mind, but I answered it. They said you were going with them to some club in Provo tonight?” Alisa said, hand on her hip.

“Oh, yeah,” he said, getting up from the bench. “I forgot about that. Guess I should call them back.”

He only looked back at Paige for an instant before going back into the house. Tears bubbled up in Paige’s throat, threatening to fall. What game was he playing? He’s going out with Becca and Lucie? But then he’s almost kissing her? And then he doesn’t say a word to her as he goes into the house? Not even, “Hey Paige, would you like to go with?” or “I’ll tell them I’m busy tonight.” He was in too much of a hurry to get to his phone.

Alisa sat herself down next to Paige.

“What was that? Was I imagining it, or did I see you kissing my brother?”

"You were imagining it," Paige said, swallowing the lump in her throat. "Seems he has more important places to be, or people to be seen with."

"Mmhmm," Alisa murmured. "I wonder why, if you're so unimportant, he talks about you all the time then. And then this." She waived her hand around. "Whatever it was I didn't see."

"It doesn't matter, Lise," Paige said, holding back tears only because she felt so angry. "He's going to some club with Tweedledee and Tweedledum. He couldn't get off the swing fast enough at their beckoning, if you didn't notice. They're way more fun than some frumpy, old schoolmarm he used to date."

Alisa put her arms around Paige's shoulders. "What is up with the men around here lately? There must be something in the water."

"And I'm sorry Tom is giving you a hard time," Paige said as she wrapped her arms around her best friend. She rested her head on her shoulder.

"I'm surprised the entire neighborhood didn't hear us," Alisa said, grimacing. "I know he's under a lot of stress with his mom and dad and the wedding. Heaven knows my mom and dad don't make it any easier. I wish he wouldn't try to pick fights with me about it."

"Well, I have two things that might make you feel better," Paige said. "I have it on good authority that Tom, regardless of the dork he's being right now, is head over heels in love with you. I'm sure he'll settle down after the wedding."

"What's the second thing?"

"We get to eat cake tomorrow. Lots of yummy cake."

Chapter 13

Paige made her way out to her car. Cake tomorrow. Everything is better with cake.

We should bring Tom, Paige thought. *He needs cake.*

She was so engrossed in getting back to her parents' home, she didn't really register people talking nearby until she glanced up. Through the windshield, she observed Becca chatting with Caleb. He looked relaxed, leaning against Becca's car. Becca put a hand on the hood of the car next to Caleb's hip and moved in closer. Paige sat frozen as, just as with any train wreck she couldn't look away from, she saw Becca say something to Caleb. Caleb bent over, and then Becca's lips were against his, kissing him.

Paige's stomach heaved. Her hand shook as she turned over the ignition and put the gearshift into drive. She looked up and locked eyes with Caleb. She sped down the road. She didn't care where she was going. She needed to get away.

She got out her cell phone.

"Hey, uh, Lise," Paige said, her voice trembling. "I won't be able to come to the cake tasting tomorrow."

"Is everything okay?"

"No. I can't make it. Take Tom and Caleb with you."

"Paige, you're freaking me out. What is going on?"

"You should ask Caleb that when he comes back in the house," Paige said, the tears dripping down her cheeks. "I'm sorry, Lise, I gotta go."

She ended the call and threw the phone onto her passenger seat. She gulped down lungful after lungful of air. She wouldn't start crying. He wasn't worth crying over. He was a single, good-looking man. He could attract and be attracted to whomever he wanted. She knew all this. She had known it before he even walked off that plane. Why should it shock her when he did exactly what she thought he would? Like any guy, he'd kiss multiple pretty women when the opportunity presented itself. He wouldn't get serious with any of them, so he was going to enjoy himself while he was here. She was just another notch on his belt to brag about when he got home to his buddies in South Carolina. She was an idiot for falling for it.

When he flew back to Beaufort the next weekend, everyone would expect their lives would go on like they had before. Hers would be on repeat, agonizingly familiar to her. She'd live her life—teach school, attend the singles' ward, and even keep dating Elliot if she wanted. Everything would seem the same until she tried to go to bed. As sure as day turns to night, his face would haunt her before she fell asleep. She'd struggled for a long time after he left to keep him out of her head, but he'd never really disappeared. She'd learned to ignore it as the visions faded slightly. The vivid memories would haunt her again. And once again, she'd think of his handsome face and feel the burn of regret.

She wiped a hand across her cheek. She would not cry. She shouldn't be sad. She should be angry. She was angry she'd fooled herself into thinking anything would be different. The occasional kindness he directed at her reminded her so much of his high school self. She was resentful toward Caleb for being devastatingly handsome, and he didn't even try to be. She was saddened because he joined the Church years after his membership would have changed the course of their lives, maybe for the better. She despised him for his teasing personality that still made her giggle. His almost-kiss alluded to kisses from him when they were together, because back then he adored and cherished her. Now, all that was tainted. His kiss obviously meant nothing to him, except how many times he got to bestow it.

She would not be led around again. The wedding was in eight days. She would survive because there were still lots of things that needed to be completed that would keep her busy. Caleb deserved the barest amount of attention. He was only the best man after all.

He wanted to hang out with Becca and make out with her? Fine. That was his prerogative, and Becca would probably be more than happy to oblige him. Paige respected herself more than that, held her men to a higher standard of conduct, and he'd proven he didn't play at that standard. She didn't associate with guys who played around with women's feelings. Caleb had Tom and Alisa to talk to and be friends with. She didn't need the extra grief.

Paige didn't go anywhere in particular. She made it as far as Hill Air Force Base before she turned around and went back to Bountiful. Her phone pinged at regular intervals and even rang a few times, but she didn't even look at the screen. If it was Alisa, then Paige would chat with her later when she wasn't so angry at her twin. If it was her parents, Paige was already headed back. If it was Lindsay, then she probably needed her to babysit, and considering today's events, that might be a pleasant distraction. If it was Caleb, he could take a flying leap off a Great Salt Lake pier and get stuck in the stinky, boggy mud and stay there.

She pulled up to her parents' house and walked through the door.

"There you are," Liz declared. "Alisa's been calling me every fifteen minutes hoping you'd be here."

"I wasn't answering my phone."

"Do you want to tell me about it?"

"Not particularly. I love Alisa and being able to be around her, but the wedding can't come soon enough. Then everything will go back to normal."

Paige walked over to the couch and lay across it. She put her arm over her eyes. Liz sat down on the space left and ran her hands through Paige's hair.

"You haven't done this in a while," Paige said, looking up at her mother.

"You need it right now," Liz replied. "It used to calm you down so quickly when you were a toddler. I remember your face would become so red, and your little foot would stomp. And I would sit there and wait until you came over to hug me. When you did, I'd stroke your hair, and you'd be fast asleep on my shoulder before I knew it."

"Thanks, Mom," Paige said, putting her arm back over her eyes. She let her mother stroke her hair for a while longer. It was comforting, and today had been such crap. The gentle caress relaxed her to sleep.

When she woke up, savory smells wafted over from the kitchen. She peered around. Liz was in the kitchen getting dinner ready.

"Mom, why didn't you wake me up? I won't be able to sleep tonight."

"You looked like you needed the rest. Alisa and you have been so busy. I spoke to her while you were asleep. She says you've been doing an expert job at keeping the peace over at the Watsons'. That can't be easy considering the circumstances."

Paige sighed. "I keep telling her that these short weeks she would be in town should only be about her and Tom. Every time I turn around lately, I'm smack dab in the middle of drama I didn't mean to create or had nothing to do with. I feel so bad."

"Do you want to talk about it now?"

Paige frowned at her mom. "If you've talked to Alisa, you already have an idea what it's about."

"That's true, but I wanted you to tell me yourself what happened. Anyone else is really just guessing."

Paige's anger flared. "Guessing? Caleb playing tonsil hockey with Becca Groves after he tried to kiss me is something they need to guess about?"

"Oh," Liz said.

"And the ludicrous thing is, Mom, I have been telling myself all week to let things lie. Caleb and I live such separate lives now. Sometimes I felt like something was there. But then he'd do or say something that proved I was totally wrong. Now I feel angry and stupid."

"I get the angry part, but I don't think you're stupid. You're my smart girl, and if anything, you miscalculated. It happens to the best of us," Liz suggested.

"Seems like a huge miscalculation. Regardless, I've decided to get through the wedding interacting with Caleb only as necessary. It's what I should have done in the first place."

"Well, I wish you good luck. You're still the maid of honor, and he's still the best man, besides being your best friend's brother. You're not going to be able to avoid him as much as you hope."

"I didn't plan on avoiding him. I just won't talk to him."

"That should be interesting since I've invited Tom, Alisa, and Caleb over for dinner tonight."

"Mom!"

"I guess you can tell Caleb about it when he arrives later. You're both adults now. You can't throw a little tantrum over a frustration and give him the silent treatment like you did in high school."

"I'll give him the silent treatment all right," Paige replied. "This isn't a minor disappointment. He's running around kissing any single female in Utah he can get his hands on. Is everyone going to give him a pass because he's a guy, or is it because he'll be going home soon?"

"You need to consider his side of it before you jump to judgment," Liz answered.

"I already allowed myself to appear stupid once today. I'm not up to letting him try to insult my intelligence further," Paige said, getting up off the couch. "And at this point, even if he has a suitable explanation for what happened, I'm still not interested. It's obvious I'm nothing more than a notch on his belt. I'll be in my room until dinner."

Paige stomped off to her room. She resisted the urge to slam her door or throw all the books on her shelf to the floor or out the window. She settled for throwing herself on her bed and staring at the ceiling.

She pulled out her cell phone and dialed Elliot's number.

"Hey, stranger," he said. "Had enough of the wedding stuff?"

"Yes, very much so," she said.

"How about dinner tomorrow night?"

"I can do that. What time do you get off work?"

"Not sure yet," he said. "I'll text you when I'm close. I can't wait to see you. Seems like a while, even though it's just been since Sunday."

Paige bit her lip. This hadn't been such a good idea after all. He sounded genuinely excited to meet with her. She placed a hand to her head. "Okay, I'll be waiting for your text."

What was she doing? Was she so desperate to get back at Caleb she was now using a nice guy like Elliot? Caleb's words accused her—*close enough to not feel lonely, but far enough away to not give him the wrong idea*. Who was giving who the wrong idea? The thought of Caleb kissing Becca mere minutes after trying to kiss her, however, made her so mad the guilt about her date with Elliot disappeared.

Chapter 14

She was leafing through one of her old books when a knock came at her bedroom door. "Come in."

Alisa stood in the doorway.

"Lise, don't stand there. Come here." Paige patted the spot on the bed beside her.

"Paige."

"I've loved that we've had this time together before the wedding. The time you have here is yours. I want you and Tom to get married and ride off into the sunset, happily ever after. That's all I've ever wanted. I just keep messing it up and I'm sorry."

"Thank you, I appreciate that," Alisa said. "But only if you go talk to Caleb about what happened today."

"Why? He's a grown man and he can do what he wants. I don't get a say in any of that. He shouldn't care what I think."

"Paige," Alisa groaned. "You can be so frustrating sometimes. Just talk to him."

"Alisa, I know you love Caleb. I did too, but I've come to accept that we're different people and want different things since high school. I can't fault him for that. I was reminded of that today."

Alisa watched Paige's face during her speech. "You're being so ridiculous. Do you know what you sound like when you're trying to convince yourself of something you don't really believe?"

"I'm not kidding, Lise," Paige replied.

"Neither am I. You get it in your head you know exactly what's going on and that's how it is."

"Okay, let me put it to you like this. I'm a bit of a control freak, I admit that. Even if I still harbored feelings for Caleb, today was a stark reminder I have no control over this situation at all. So, I'm letting the things I can't control go. I'm trying to recognize even if I wanted matters to turn out a certain way, they probably won't, and that maybe they shouldn't. It should hurt less."

Alisa looked down at her hands as if struggling to say something. "Would you at least do him the courtesy of letting him explain his side?"

Paige leaned her head back. "I'm not sure I want to hear his side because it won't matter what his reasons are. Nothing will change because I don't want to care anymore."

"Please? I love both of you. I want both of you to be happy. Or at least not fighting. It's been bad enough having to dodge volleys from my parents for myself and Tom."

Alisa paused and ran her hand under her nose. She sniffed a little. "I still haven't met his parents yet, and that's a whole other can of worms that seems to want to explode right before the wedding. I'm exhausted, Paige. I just want there to be as much peace around me as possible, because it certainly doesn't exist at my house. I need peace, and I can't have it if you're mad at each other. I realize I've leaned on both of you a lot over these last few days, but I feel like I don't have a choice. You two are the only ones I can count on besides Tom."

Paige wrapped her arms around her friend. "Lise, we both want to be here for you. To help you and hold you up when you don't think you have the strength. That's how much we both love you. Caleb and I could do that even if we weren't talking to each other, but I understand what you're trying to say. I'd do anything for you. You know that. I know

Caleb would throw himself over an IED for anyone, but most especially you. If you want me to talk to him, I will. I can't promise things will get better, but I'll do it."

"Thank you," Alisa sighed. "I'm glad your parents invited us over for supper. It'll be nice to eat in peace for once."

The two women left Paige's room and made their way to the kitchen and the dining area. Paige pulled out the dishes and silverware and set up the table for dinner. She ignored everything else. For Alisa, she would talk to Caleb. Paige would have refused outright had anyone else asked her, and Alisa knew it. She still had no idea why it was so important for her to talk to him. Whatever he had to say wouldn't matter. She was done. She'd gotten a hard dose of reality this afternoon, and, like she told Alisa, she didn't want to care anymore. She'd been fooling herself this whole time into hoping Caleb could feel anything more for her.

Even if what Caleb said didn't matter, Paige was still curious how he planned on explaining himself. There was no way she could have misinterpreted what she saw. You don't lean over and kiss someone and claim it was an accident. He'd wanted to kiss Becca. That had been obvious or he would have stopped it. But again, she had to remind herself he didn't need to justify that either. He could kiss Becca all he wanted. Paige wasn't going to allow herself to be roped in again by his good looks and be made to look the fool. She wasn't as desperate for his attention as all that.

Liz carefully orchestrated it so Paige and Caleb sat next to each other at the dinner table. Wally said the blessing and shrewdly inserted a request for the Spirit to overcome contention. He only smiled at her when she shot him a dirty look.

Everyone but Paige and Caleb conversed pleasantly with each other. Paige did little more than push her food around, and Caleb acted like his dinner was his last meal.

"Mom, that was great. Thanks," Paige said, standing up. "Caleb, would you mind joining me outside, please?"

"Thanks for dinner, Brother and Sister Ellis," he said before leaving the table and following Paige out to the backyard.

Paige paced the edge of the cement patio, arms folded. She thought about how to start. She didn't want to go in guns blazing, but she saw through him and she wanted him to realize that.

"Alisa said you needed to tell me whatever it is you plan on telling me," Paige said after he shut the patio door behind him. "But before you do, I wanted to acknowledge that we're both adults. We're not dating in high school anymore. Whatever it is I saw, I don't care. It was none of my business to begin with."

Caleb walked up to stand directly in front of her. She had to look up at him to look him in the eyes. "You're so full of crap."

Paige's temper flared. "Funny. I could have said the same thing about you, but I was trying to be reasonable and nice."

"What do you want me to say, Paige? I leaned over to hear something Becca tried to tell me, and she kissed me on the mouth. It just happened."

Paige nodded in mock agreement. "I guess the fact that you were trying to kiss me only minutes before that had nothing to do with it. Was your notch quota low for the day?"

He leaned forward toward her. The smug look on his striking face made her want to smack him. "Is this what this is about? Feeling a little jealous, Paige?"

"You wish. You would just love to stroke your ego with that one, wouldn't you, Caleb? But jealousy implies that I actually care."

He laughed out loud. The deep sound vibrated throughout her body giving her chills long after he'd finished laughing. "You're so green with jealousy I should call you the wicked witch."

She stepped up to him and pointed a finger toward his face. "Believe what you want. I don't care. All I've been trying to say is go ahead and do whatever with my blessing. You're going to anyway. But you must admit a high kill count out here in Utah will be a nice bragging point for your buddies back in South Carolina. It's so juvenile, and I don't want any part of it."

The aura of his cologne, and his warmth was like a magnetic force, and as much as her brain screamed at her to step back, she'd gotten too close and now she was caught. Her nerves fired off every time a part of him moved but especially when his eyes kept flicking from her own eyes to her mouth and back.

He pushed her wrist out of the way. He hung over her like some heaving, colossal monolith that radiated heat. "Juvenile? You're the one that flipped out instead of acting like a grown-up. You go running off, no one can find you, you don't answer your phone and all because you saw me kissing someone else. You run away and act jealous and you have the nerve to call me juvenile? What's the real deal here, Paige? Why do you care so much? Don't try and tell me you don't."

Paige sucked in a breath trying not to let anymore of his heady aroma invade her head. "Nice try, Caleb. I've been trying to tell you since we started this conversation, I don't care who you do anything with. I had no say in that before you came back to Utah—I don't have any say now."

Caleb pressed in farther, however, pushing her right up against the concrete edge. He put his face right in hers.

"All right. Fine. I'll take you at your word. Becca, unlike *some others*, wants to hang out with me and include me. That's more than some can say. We're still going to the club tonight. I had planned on inviting you too, but someone drove off in a huff before I got a chance to."

"Well, gee, how noble of you for thinking of me and taking pity. No thanks. I can think of a hundred things more fun than hanging out with a girl who was barely out of diapers when we hit high school."

"Oh!" he exclaimed, throwing his head backward and laughing. "That is what this is all about. I wish I had seen it sooner. I might not have felt as bad as I did."

"What are you talking about?"

"Feeling a little out of your league amongst Becca's age group, Paige?" he murmured at her, his smirk spreading across his face.

"The only concern I had about Becca was that you couldn't get chummy with her fast enough despite the nearly full-decade age difference, like any other typical male."

"I wish you would come out and say it. This is such a waste of time," he said. "Say, 'I'm feeling like an old maid living here in Utah, because I'm not married yet and nearly thirty.' "

Paige gasped as the words struck a nerve. She turned, scrunching her eyes as hard as she could. She wouldn't give him the satisfaction of letting him see her cry. At that moment, any desire for his forgiveness evaporated. She bit her lip. Alisa wanted her to make peace with Caleb. She didn't see how she could do that now. His smugness overwhelmed her.

His warm presence came right up and pressed against her back. "I'm sorry, Paige. I don't know what made me say that."

His hands turned her around. She wiped away the few tears that had escaped her eyes before she looked up into his troubled face. His mouth moved like he wanted to say something but wasn't sure what. He was so close Paige found it hard to breathe, especially since his hands had gone from holding her arms to wrapping themselves around her trembling body. He looked over her face, his eyes ending at her mouth. She parted her lips to take in a small breath to keep from passing out entirely.

His lips came down on hers. She breathed in and held it for a moment before she realized that he was in earnest. Her knees buckled under the sudden onslaught of emotion, and she encircled his neck with her arms. The feel of his kiss on her lips was so familiar, but different. Familiar because his natural smell was the same. His technique had improved, but he still savored her mouth slowly and sweetly like he had in high school. Different because she had to reach up farther to get her arms around his neck. It allowed her to drape herself on him, closing any gap between them. Her heart raced, leaning against his broad chest and adoring the feeling of his sturdy arms wrapped around her—he was not a teenager anymore.

The word *teenager* pulled her brain out of the fog of desire she found herself in. She jerked her head back and looked at him. What was she doing? He'd just admitted he preferred Becca's company. He'd called her an old maid. Did he really think a kiss was going to make up for his ridicule? Her jaw clenched and her stomach sank at the same time. So much for caring—she didn't need sympathy from him. If he thought one kiss would erase the sickening sight of his face against Becca's, he needed to think again.

SMACK

The sound echoed in the nighttime's silence as her hand connected with his cheek.

"How dare you," she said. She marched toward the house. "You must think I'm some big joke if you think you can mess with my head so easily. This old maid's not so impressed by a head-turning kiss these days—like Becca may be."

She walked into the house and swept past everyone in the living room. As she moved by Alisa, she growled, "I'll see you at the cake tasting tomorrow." She went straight to her room and slammed the door. She collapsed against it and slid to the floor, then held her head in her hands and cried.

Chapter 15

Paige, Tom, Alisa and Caleb sat in the café area of the small bakery. Paige kept peering over at Alisa who kept glancing over at Caleb, and Tom watched everyone. A palpable silence sat in the air. Alisa sighed.

"Would you gentleman excuse us for a moment? Babe, tell Marnie we'll be right back if she comes," Alisa said, gripping Paige by the wrist and hauling her to her feet. "We need to use the bathroom to wash our hands."

There was a slight emphasis on *hands* as Alisa dragged Paige to the restroom.

When the door was shut and locked, Alisa whirled around on Paige.

"Tell me exactly what happened last night," she said, eyeing Paige like a hawk.

"I slapped him," Paige answered.

"You slapped him?"

"Yup."

"Why?"

"Apparently, he thought that he could call me things like 'old maid' and kiss me and make it all better."

"He kissed you?"

"He didn't tell you?" Paige sighed angrily. "Of course he didn't. Getting another notch on his belt to brag about to his buddies isn't something he'd want to tell his sister."

"Now hold on," Alisa said. "You can say a lot of things about him in front of me, but he's never been that kind of guy."

"Yeah, right," Paige murmured, folding her arms. Alisa glared at Paige. "So, yes, I admit we almost kissed in your parents' backyard but we didn't. But that would have only made what happened worse. I walk outside not ten minutes later and there he is locking lips with Becca. Explain to me how that's not being that kind of guy? Last night I asked him what game he was playing when he tried to kiss me in your backyard then minutes later kissed Becca. He told me Becca surprised him with the kiss but he didn't see it as a big deal. Then accused me of being jealous. I was in the middle of correcting him when he actually kissed me. The slap was to remind him I'm not Becca's age anymore, and he can't make me forget his crappy behavior with a kiss of his."

"What did he say after that?"

"Nothing. I didn't give him a chance to say anything. I came in the house. I didn't appreciate being manipulated."

"I think you're giving him too much credit for using his brain constructively when he's kissing someone."

Paige scoffed.

"You should know as well as I do that my brother is many things, but Machiavellian is not one of them," Alisa replied. "He's straightforward and honest. If he told you he wasn't playing games with you or Becca, or that he felt nothing kissing Becca, then he didn't."

"And I think you don't want to believe him capable of something like that," Paige said, her hands fisting at her sides.

"Paige, you haven't been around him for the last ten years," Alisa said. "I have. My twin is an honest and good man, and he doesn't treat women like that. He's changed in a lot of ways, but there are some things that haven't changed since high school. He never once acted like that in the high school we went to before we moved. He certainly never tried that stuff when he was dating you. And let me assure you, there were plenty of girls at

Bountiful High that would have loved to see you two break up. If you recall, you never had to worry about him looking at other girls because he never gave you a reason, did he?"

Alisa gave Paige a pointed stare and waited. Paige swallowed. Suddenly her hands were extremely interesting and she couldn't look at Alisa.

"You're right," Paige said. "He was never like that when he was with me."

"Now, can we please have a second's worth of peace between you two?"

"Yes. As far as I'm concerned. I'll even do you one better. I will apologize for slapping him. Doesn't matter what he did. I shouldn't have done that, anyway."

"Okay," Alisa said, giving Paige a light hug. "It's why I love you. There are occasions where I can talk reason to you. Let's go try out this cake."

The two women returned to the table and sat down. Paige glanced up at Caleb. He watched her sitting there but said nothing.

"You're back!" Marnie said, coming up to their table. "Let me go get the samples. I've made it so you can mix and match the cake, frostings, and fillings, so let me know which combination you like best."

"Can't wait!" Alisa said, rubbing her hands together.

Paige moved her chair closer to Caleb's.

"I wanted to apologize for last night," she murmured to him. He leaned his head toward her, listening. "I shouldn't have slapped you. And I wasn't giving you lip service when I said you're free to do whatever you want because it's none of my business. It's true. I believe that, but I overreacted, anyway."

She stared at the tabletop. She waited for a response from him, but she prepared herself in case she didn't get one. He had a right to be mad at her, about several things. She hadn't done herself any favors with her behavior last night.

"I was worried I might wake up this morning with a nice red mark on my face," he murmured back.

He pointed to the offended cheek. It looked normal.

"But, thankfully, you hit like a girl," he replied, then leaned back in his chair.

Paige almost snorted as she struggled to hold back her giggle. She wanted to stomp her foot. She was struggling to be serious, but there he was trying to make her laugh. At least he wasn't mad. That felt good for once. It still irritated her he had been a jerk last week, but at least, for the moment, things were settled. "I guess in this case, it's a relief to know."

Marnie came back with a tray that had finger slices of different cakes. She'd also included little ramekins of frosting and filling with mini spoons for them to try.

"You've got your standard chocolate and white cakes, then I've also added lemon, strawberry, carrot, red velvet, and dark chocolate. Then for frostings you've got vanilla bean and chocolate, white chocolate, German chocolate, cream cheese, whipped raspberry, and chocolate ganache. For fillings, I've got the standard fruit jellies, salted caramel, and for fun, cookies and cream. These are my most popular, but if you have a particular flavor you've heard of, I'll see if I can whip you up a sample. Just let me know!"

Alisa headed straight for the chocolate cake and loaded it up with German chocolate frosting.

"Please, baby, no coconut," Tom said, looking pained.

"Aww," Alisa said, as she stuffed the slice in her mouth. "But it's so good!"

Paige giggled. "I'm trying the lemon. That looks like a good flavor for a summer wedding."

She picked up the light yellow cake and surveyed the frosting options. She took the small spoon for the whipped raspberry and spread it neatly over the slice. The combination of the sweet tartness of the raspberry frosting fusing with the zing of the lemon in the cake melted in her mouth.

"Oh, my gosh, that was so good," Paige exclaimed. "Lise, you really need to try this combo."

"This carrot with the cream cheese is fantastic," Caleb said, showing everyone his slice. The cake had a caramel brown color with rich, dark pieces of raisin and walnut. It looked exactly like the kind Paige's grandmother served when Paige was younger.

"That looks fantastic. Can I have a bite?" Paige asked.

"Of this?" Caleb asked, holding up his piece.

"Yes," Paige answered. "I don't want a whole slice. I just want a small bite to see if it tastes like my grandma's carrot cake."

"Okay, as long as I can have a bit of yours," he replied. "I'm not totally sold on lemon-flavored cake, but it's worth a bite."

He broke a good-sized chunk off from the end, and held it up to her mouth. Suddenly, the thought hit her. This whole arrangement was way too much like exchanging bites at a reception. She didn't know if she should giggle or let her stomach churn itself into knots. She leaned in and attempted to take the bite, but his hand jerked, and she got a nose full of cream cheese frosting.

"Hey!" she complained. "Thanks for getting frosting all over me, Caleb."

She tried wiping it off with a napkin.

"Sorry, my hand twitched," he tried declaring innocently, but his eyes danced.

"Likely story," she grumbled. "Did I get it all?"

She showed her face to him.

"Here, let me," he said, taking the napkin from her. He wiped around her nose area, but he was taking way too long for a mere second-over.

"All right, I believe you got it," she said, waving his hand away. "Did you still want a bite?"

"Sure," he replied, his lips twitching.

As she held the bite up for him, Alisa looked over at Paige. "What's all over your face?"

Paige pulled in a gasp. "I knew it!" She took her slice and shoved it into his face. She grabbed her napkin. "Here, Caleb, can I help you clean that up?" She tried attacking his face, but he grabbed her wrists to fend her off.

"That was cheap, even for you, Paige," he said. He let go of one of her wrists. His hand rummaged around the table until it connected with cake, and she was suddenly showered in red velvet and chocolate.

"Oh, you're so dead," she said. She reached over and grabbed a ramekin of white chocolate frosting and jumped halfway into his lap to push the frosting cup onto his cheek.

"You guys!" Alisa exclaimed while Tom sat back and laughed his head off. "You're going to get us kicked out! Tom, this isn't funny!"

"This is hilarious," he said. "I need to take pictures."

Caleb got ahold of a ramekin of frosting. Chocolate ganache dripped off Paige's chin before she could grab a handful of the dark chocolate and strawberry cakes. She shoved the cake in Caleb's mouth and kept her hand there.

Caleb laughed so hard and leaned back so far to avoid the cake, the chair tipped backward dangerously.

"Woah!" they both exclaimed, as Paige grabbed Caleb around the neck to keep from falling. Only Caleb's long legs kept them from tipping over entirely, and he got the chair upright again. Paige collapsed onto Caleb's shoulder, both of them laughing until she felt like she couldn't breathe.

"What the—?" Marnie said, as she came back into the café. Paige jumped up off of him and started to brush off crumbs of cake that were everywhere on her clothes.

"I guess we need a broom," Caleb said. "Paige dropped some cake on the floor."

Paige smacked him on the shoulder. He couldn't hold back his giggles as he tried to protect the offended shoulder.

"I think we'll need a washcloth too," Paige suggested. "Caleb got some frosting on his face."

Alisa inspected them both with a mixture of chagrin and amusement.

"Can't take you guys anywhere," Alisa said, shaking her head. "Even now. Geez."

Marnie came back from the kitchen to hand the guilty pair the implements they asked for, giving them each a peeved stare. While Tom and Alisa finished deciding what cake they wanted for the wedding, Paige and Caleb cleaned up their mess.

"And you guys accused me of getting you in trouble all the time," Caleb replied. "My, my, how times have changed."

"I didn't purposely get frosting all over your face until after you did it to me," Paige said. "You deserved it."

"Maybe," he said, grinning. "But it was hilarious."

Tom's cell phone rang. "I'll take this while you two finish up and Alisa puts in the order. Behave!" He pointed to the both of them.

Caleb held his hands up in mock innocence.

Alisa inspected the job they'd done. "That's better. I expect this of Caleb, but you, Paige?"

"He started it," Paige said, pointing at him.

Tom moved to the back of the bakery with his phone to his ear.

"Yes, sir," he answered. "We'd be happy to. It'll be good to see you and your wife again. Oh, no, that is so generous of you already. Okay, I'll talk to my fiancé, and I'll let you know. You too, sir.

"Babe, do you know who that was? That was Colonel Martin," Tom said. He looked at Paige. "He was in the branch presidency when Caleb and Alisa were first baptized. Alisa, are we doing anything this weekend for the wedding?"

"No, everything that can be done before next week is done," Alisa said. "What did he want?"

"He retired a couple of years ago to some place up north called Logan. He just called because he and his wife won't be able to come to the wedding, but they wanted to invite us up to visit them this weekend."

"That sounds nice," Alisa replied.

“Better than nice. I was telling him we didn’t have a bachelor’s party planned, and he says we can take his boat onto Bear Lake for the 4th of July.”

“Oh, that sounds like a lot of fun! A bachelor/bachelorette party? How many people can we invite?” Alisa asked.

“He said as many people as we want. He said there’s a ton of room to put people in his house. Not sure how many would fit on his boat at one time, though. There’s one caveat. We have to take Sergeant Benning with us.”

“As in, Henry Benning?” Caleb asked.

“Colonel Martin is his uncle, and he’s living with them while he goes to Utah State for poli-sci.”

“That shouldn’t be a problem,” Caleb said. “He’s a good guy. It’ll be fun to have a bunch of us from Beaufort together.”

“Did you guys forget one thing?” Alisa asked. “He’s painfully shy. He may not have any fun.”

“Eh, he probably grew out of it,” Caleb said. “Why would a guy be majoring in political science if he can’t talk to anyone? It was mostly around girls, anyway.”

Alisa rolled her eyes.

“When are we leaving?” Paige asked.

“Is tomorrow too soon?” Tom asked.

“I have a date tonight with Elliot,” Paige replied. “Other than that, my calendar is wide open until the 10th.”

Paige glanced over at Caleb. His jaw twitched as the lightness in his face faded.

“Good, I’d like to get up there so we have some time to visit with the colonel and his wife before we hit the lake.”

“We should talk more about this when we get home,” Alisa declared. “I assume we’ve more than worn out our welcome here.”

Paige smiled at Marnie and brought her the broom and wash cloth. "The lemon cake was amazing. Especially with the raspberry frosting."

Marnie took the compliment in good grace but looked more than a little relieved when the group left.

Chapter 16

Alisa's cheerful mood was infectious as they headed back to her parents' house. Paige loved to see it.

"I think I've only ever been to Bear Lake once," Alisa said. "And we weren't on a boat that time. Just along the shoreline. This is going to be so much fun. Do you think it will be crowded because it's the 4th?"

Paige was about to answer her when she saw Becca's car parked in front of the Watsons'.

"Were you expecting Becca and Lucie, Caleb?" Alisa asked, looking back at her brother.

"No, but it's fine. We'll find something to do," he stated.

Alisa glanced over at Paige, but all Paige did was roll her eyes. Let him torture himself if that's what he wanted.

When they walked through the door of the house, Becca and Lucie sat talking with Karen.

"Hi!" Becca said, jumping up and waving. "You guys took forever."

"Why didn't you text and say you were over here?" Caleb asked.

Becca shrugged. "We talked to your mom while we waited."

Paige's eyebrows shot into her hairline. Karen was barely civil to Tom or Paige, but she welcomed the Groves girls she knew very well were Mormon too? Paige didn't understand her sometimes.

"Mom, we've been invited up to Logan this weekend. An old commanding officer of Caleb and Tom's can't come to the wedding and wants to see us," Alisa said, approaching her mother. "We should be home by Sunday afternoon. It'll give you guys a few days to yourselves before the wedding."

"Whatever you want to do," Karen said, sounding almost defeated. "Did you need anything going up?"

"We'll need to borrow one of the cars."

"Talk to your dad about the keys and insurance," Karen said, turning to go to the back bedrooms.

Becca and Lucie started jumping up and down, clapping. "Can we come? That sounds like so much fun!"

"Um, I suppose you could," Alisa said, glancing at Paige. "Can you be ready to leave by tomorrow morning?"

"Yeah, that'd be easy," Becca said.

"Okay, so Paige and I, Tom and Caleb, Lucie and Becca, and Henry," Alisa said. "That's seven total. Would we need to invite Elliot, Paige?"

"I doubt he'd be able to take the day off on such short notice if we're leaving tomorrow," Paige replied.

"So, seven. That's not too bad. And Sister Martin's got room for all of us?"

"That's what the colonel said."

"Come on, Caleb," Becca said, grabbing onto his arm and pulling him toward the front door. "Lucie and I have a surprise for you."

"I'm going in the backyard to see if I can get ahold of Benning," Tom said, kissing Alisa before opening the patio door.

Paige ground her teeth. As soon as Alisa and Paige were alone, Paige pounced on Alisa.

"Really?"

"What did you want me to do? They were standing there, begging to go."

"Say no?"

"I did you a favor. They'd tell Brent, and then Lindsay would let you hear all about it. She's probably going out of her mind with them around all the time."

Paige sighed. "I'm just tired of watching Becca throw herself at Caleb."

"You know," Alisa said, giving Paige a side glance. Her tone was too self-satisfied. "There's one way you could fix that situation super fast."

"How?"

"Stop being so prideful and stubborn and tell Caleb how you feel for real. No dancing around it anymore. Just say it."

"What are you talking about?"

"You know very well what I'm talking about, Paige Ellis. You don't fool me in the slightest. I've been watching you around each other these past couple of weeks."

"I guess I missed seeing what you're seeing. All he's done this whole time is parade his bestest buddy Becca around, call me names like *old maid,* and act like a jerk. For all I know, he'd smugly throw it back to me then brag about his plans to get engaged to Becca for good measure."

Alisa's face was a mix of anger and disapproval. "First, he wouldn't do something as cruel as that to anyone, least of all, you. Besides, Becca's IQ isn't high enough for him. Second, as his sister and twin, I'm sure he's still as much in love with you as you are with him."

"Lise, don't say that. That doesn't make any of this easier."

"Deny it all you want, but I know the truth. My brother and you deserve each other. He's as pig-headed as you are. And the worst part is I think he knows what he wants, but he's doing exactly what you're doing. He's nitpicking the situation, and he's waiting for you to make the first move."

"What?"

Alisa looked Paige directly in the eye. Paige put her head in her hands.

"I can't do it, Lise," Paige said, her chest heaving as she struggled to keep her emotions under control. "I know I'm not an innocent party in all of this. I've done some really stupid things. But I won't let him have that kind of power over my heart, especially when he hasn't done anything that says he wants it. I can't be that broken again. Not when it's just a gut feeling for you. I realize it's something you might hope for but it's an awfully big thing you're asking me to do. I will not put myself out there only to find out you've misjudged how he feels about me."

"Paige, I love you both. I also know you both really well. I would never send you on a fool's errand just because I hope for something. But I also can't force you to do anything, and it frustrates me to see you guys walking away from something that's so obvious to just about everyone else but you two. Something's got to give. If it doesn't, you'll both go on being miserable for the next ten years."

"Then I'll have to keep being miserable. It's not just about being unsure of his feelings either. You can't have love if you don't have forgiveness. He still hasn't forgiven me for the last time. Did I tell you I tried apologizing last week for what happened on graduation night? He didn't say a thing afterward, and he's never brought it up since. That's all I can do. I can't force him to accept my apology, so I'm forced to live with the choices I made back then. It's been so hard to think that if I had made different choices back then, we wouldn't be having this conversation now. He and I would probably have eight kids by now or something."

"Eight?"

"You know what I mean."

"I don't know why he hasn't brought your apology back up. He hasn't talked to me about it. He has to understand the reasons you rejected him back then. I don't see how he couldn't because I finally understand why, now that I'm a member. You're assuming he's not willing to forgive you. I'm saying maybe he hasn't had a chance to say it. And you do have the habit of cutting people off when you don't want to hear what they have to say—when you're afraid of the answer. Maybe you haven't given him the chance because you're mistaking it for something else."

"I hate this. Why does this have to be so confusing and complicated?"

"You are both making this way more complicated than it has to be because you're both being stubborn. And then you're both not helping anything by being stupid with other people. You with Elliot and him with Becca," Alisa said. "You and Caleb need to have a heart to heart sometime in the next week. Otherwise, you may never have another chance."

"Then I may never get another chance. I can't put myself out there just in case he forgave me, or happens to have fallen in love with me again. I can't get my heart broken again that deeply."

Alisa rubbed Paige's arm. "I wish there was something more I could say that would make you believe everything will be all right. It's hard being in love. It's so amazing and wonderful, but sometimes it hurts too." Paige could tell Alisa was trying to suppress her worry.

"I'm so glad Brother Martin called. Tom needs this weekend away," Paige replied. "Let's go and have fun playing in the water. Get away from the stress. Mentally prepare for the big day."

"I agree. He needs it," Alisa said, sighing. "Both his parents confirmed they're coming, and that hasn't helped the amount of stress he's under."

"Then no more drama until we get back."

"Everyone is leading me to an early grave, just saying."

"I'm going home to pack. Then I'm going out on this date with Elliot and look forward to the weekend," Paige said. In a ditzy voice, she said, "It will be super-much fun with Tweedledee and Tweedledum around." She flipped her hair over her shoulder.

"Spoil sport," Alisa said. "You have one thing both the Groves girls don't have combined."

"What's that?"

"More than ten brain cells."

Paige tried so hard to keep from laughing aloud she snorted.

Paige watched Elliot pull up to the restaurant. He looked surprised to see her.

"You're on time," he said, smiling.

Paige blushed. "Yeah, well, I figured it would be unforgivable of me to continue to make you wait for me all the time. You haven't complained—even so, it makes me feel bad."

"I'm just glad you're here," he replied. He led her into the restaurant. He smiled across the table at her after helping her with her chair.

"So, how are the wedding plans coming?"

"Everything's ready as they can be," Paige answered. "It's an immense relief. Now we can just concentrate on spending time with each other and catching up. How did your company party go?"

"It went well," he answered. "Do you remember Jennifer Hardy from the ward?"

"I think so. She's that tall blonde gal in the Relief Society Presidency, right?"

"Right. She went with me, and we had a good time. Probably not as much as you and I would have had, but fun."

Paige tried to mask her mix of irritation and amusement at his statement with a smile. "Oh, good. She is a really friendly person. We're not that well acquainted, but she's always been nice to me. I'm glad you had fun with her."

"What are your plans for this weekend?" he asked. "Maybe we can hike up to the Y on the mountain and watch the Stadium of Fire fireworks?"

"Oh, about that," Paige replied. "Alisa and her fiancé were invited to visit a former boss of Tom and Caleb's this weekend in Logan. We'll be up at Bear Lake. It was all very last minute since the colonel and his wife won't be able to come to the wedding. We were going to invite you. I didn't think you'd be able to get the time off so quickly since we're leaving tomorrow morning."

"You're right. I wouldn't," he said, looking slightly disappointed. "But I appreciate you thinking of me."

Yes, that would have been nice of her. Too bad it was actually Alisa that thought of him at all

"You'll be back on Sunday though, right?" he asked.

"That's the plan," Paige said. "I'm not sure if we'll make it back in time for church, but we'll try our best."

He nodded. "I hope you have fun up in Logan, then. What are your plans for after the wedding?"

"I can only guess I'll be prepping for next school year. August is the month of school meetings and classroom prep with my TA," she said.

"I'm at your disposal anytime on the weekends. I'd be happy to come hang things up for you."

"That's sweet of you to offer. I imagine your height could come in handy. You and Caleb are about the same height. I couldn't touch the top of his head even if I stretched up on my tiptoes."

Elliot colored a bit, and Paige shut her mouth. Seemed she just couldn't pass up an opportunity to mention Caleb tonight.

"So, um, I'm thinking of doing a unit on important helpers in the community this upcoming year," she said. "We'd do a report on a community hero like a firefighter or police officer. Maybe even the military . . . But anyway, you could come talk to the kids as my special guest."

"A lawyer is a hero?" Elliot asked, amused.

"Sure," Paige suggested. "You help people solve disputes."

Elliot laughed. "I never thought about it like that, but if you want me to, I'll come. Just let me know when."

Their dinner came, and the inevitable silence overtook the table. She took a peek at Elliot when he wasn't looking. Her life would be so much easier if she felt anything for him beyond friendship. Elliot was more than interested. If she gave Elliot even the slightest encouragement, there'd probably be a ring from him in her future. But she didn't want it. Some other girl, someday, would be extremely lucky to be getting herself such a man. That realization only made her feel even more like she was using Elliot. She had him take her out, not because she wanted to go out with him necessarily, but because she'd wanted to get back at Caleb. And just like any other time she tried getting back at Caleb, it was failing spectacularly. Right now, Caleb was probably with Tweedledee and Tweedledum doing something fun. Becca's hands were probably all over him, maybe even her lips, and he was blissfully unconcerned that Paige was off with Elliot having a nice dinner.

After dinner was over, Elliot walked her to her car.

"I guess I'll see you after I get back from the weekend," Paige said.

"I certainly hope so, Paige." He leaned in and Paige gave him the only consolation prize she was willing to—a kiss on the cheek.

As she drove home, she chastised herself. She really needed to be up front with Elliot, but what would she say? After Caleb flew home and Alisa and Tom were on their honeymoon, she could continue to see him, but the desire wasn't there anymore. And that was the hardest reason to explain to someone without coming across like a total jerk. *"Sorry, Elliot, you're boring even though you're a super nice guy. The most I feel is a kinship similar to what I'd feel for a cousin, or a brother, if I had one."* She put her head in her hand. It would be a conversation she would dread having.

Chapter 17

The next morning everyone stood outside the Watsons'. They had stuffed both cars with everyone's things for the weekend.

"So, who's going where?" Tom asked.

"Caleb is coming with us in his parents' car," Becca said. "You guys can go in Paige's car."

"I guess it's settled," Caleb said, looking at Paige.

"I suppose so," Paige replied. She turned to the engaged couple. "Does anyone want to drive, or should I? Actually, Tom, why don't you drive? I'm going to veg in the backseat."

Caleb came up to them and touched Paige's elbow. "Can I talk to you for a minute?"

Paige walked away from the group and turned to Caleb.

"I was hoping we could take a minute to talk about some things," he said.

"Right now? When we're getting ready to leave?"

"Yes."

"What about?"

"What are we? Are we friends? Nothing? Something else?"

Paige blinked. Her heart started pounding. "Friends?"

He scratched the back of his neck. "Okay, I needed to make sure because things seem to be getting confused. We're friends but then why haven't we planned to do anything together really?"

"Yes, somewhere the signals are getting mixed. I never said I didn't want to hang out with you, but to me it seemed like you automatically assumed that I didn't. You spend all your time with Tweedledee and Tweedledum while Alisa, your mom, and I have done all the heavy lifting for this wedding. It's not like you've been around to ask."

Caleb nodded. "I just can't seem to shake this idea that something else is going on because of the whole Becca thing the other day. Am I wrong?"

Paige's gut clenched and she folded her arms across her torso. This wasn't the place she wanted to have this conversation. She thought about what Alisa had said yesterday, and fear iced her insides over.

"Caleb, I really wish you would believe me when I try to acknowledge that you're a grown man and can do what you want with who you want. I don't get to have a say in that. It won't matter in a week anyway. You'll date whoever in South Carolina, and I'll date whoever here, maybe Elliot, maybe not."

"As much as you say you're indifferent to this Elliot guy, you seem to relish your time together," Caleb said, smirking though there was no amusement in his eyes.

"I have been on one date with him since you got back to Utah. One! You were off doing something else anyway, so why would it matter to you what I was doing?"

Caleb looked like he was about to say something else but Paige reached out and grabbed his hand. "Look. Let's just move forward, okay? Let's have a wonderful time at Bear Lake. We'll loosen up Tom, which will loosen up Alisa."

"That sounds like a reasonable suggestion to me," he said, squeezing her hand. "And can we agree to move forward as friends?"

"I'm down for that," Paige replied, pulling her hand back. Holding his hand just sent warm tingles up her arm that made the whole conversation more difficult. "I don't like fighting with you, contrary to what it looks like. I like you much more when we're laughing. Always have."

Paige's heart skipped a few beats when he gave her a crooked grin. A part of Paige was tired of dodging his obvious attempts at getting her to admit how she felt. Mostly, she felt she was doing the right thing. They had their own worlds they lived in that didn't include each other. If she laid it out bare, then she'd have her answer. There'd be no more wondering, but the answer could be as easily devastating as it was wonderful. Using up what felt like the last of her courage with him, she opened her mouth to say something, but before she could get the words out, Becca ran up to Caleb.

"Come on. Let's get out of here," she said, pulling on his forearm.

Caleb turned to look at her. "What were you going to say?"

"I'll talk to you when we get to Logan," she answered. Despair and relief flooded her. She could avoid it for now. She smiled and waved at him before opening the back door to her car. "Have fun riding with the Groves girls."

She heard an annoyed sigh as she got in.

Paige sat in the backseat playing on her phone as Tom drove the car north. Tom and Alisa held hands as they talked. Paige smiled. Everything she'd learned about him in the short time she'd known him made her more and more excited for Alisa. It said something that both the Watson siblings loved him as much as they did. He'd helped them come to the gospel, and he was Caleb's buddy before that. But more than those—he was going to make an excellent husband for Alisa.

Though she would never say so, Alisa had always wanted the type of adoration that she'd seen between Caleb and Paige. She needed and wanted someone to chase her and want her. Alisa never had anyone like that. Paige suspected Alisa had felt left out in high school because Paige and Caleb had been so close. That was hard because they couldn't help the way they felt for each other, and they hadn't purposely tried to exclude her. They probably included her more than most high school couples would have. Still, it wouldn't have been easy for her being on the outside. Harder still, when it was your beloved brother adoring and spoiling your best friend with attention. Now Alisa had Tom.

If she had faith in Alisa, then Paige had to believe she could have Caleb again. The conversation she and Caleb had before leaving replayed in her head. What was the worst that could happen should she decide to bare her soul to him one more time? The worst would be he would thank her kindly but ultimately shoot her down. It was nothing different from what she expected. It would also be a similar outcome to what would happen if she just let him go home after the wedding. Their lives would move on much as they had before, with regret and loneliness as companions.

What if she admitted the kiss and all their time together had come to mean more to her, but scared her senseless? Could she tell him the idea of him flying home to South Carolina in a week was getting less and less palatable as the wedding got closer? What was the best outcome? If Alisa was right, Caleb was still in love with her. Paige would get what she secretly longed for all these years—him.

Paige drifted off to sleep. The next thing she knew, Tom had parked the car and gotten out. She looked up. The sizeable house looked to be in an older section of Logan, built when houses had enormous yards and ancient shade trees. The gabling of the roof and the gingerbread on the wrap-around porch was captivating.

"I'd love to have a house like this," Paige said.

"It's beautiful," Alisa said. "South Carolinian houses are a lot like these. They're all structurally beautiful and have enormous magnolia trees covered in Spanish moss in the yard."

Alisa waved as Caleb's car pulled up behind theirs. Becca and Lucie hopped out. "This house is gigantic!"

Caleb came up to Tom, and they walked up to the front door together. A skinny old man appeared, but as soon as he opened the door, both Caleb and Tom snapped to attention with crisp salutes.

"At ease, Marines. It's wonderful to see you both." He pulled each man into a hug, patting them on the back.

"Sir, you remember my fiancé, Alisa Watson," Tom said, pulling Alisa up onto the porch.

"I sure do. How are you? What made you say yes to this young Marine?"

"I'm not sure, but I'm glad I did. He's a good man." She smiled over at her future husband and squeezed his hand.

"And who else did you bring with you?" Colonel Martin asked.

"This is Alisa's best friend, Paige Ellis," Caleb said.

The old man's eyes lit up, almost as if he recognized her. "Welcome. I've heard quite a bit about you."

"Thank you," Paige said, glancing at Caleb. He had just looked away, but she couldn't help but notice the slight smile on his face.

"And these two are Lucie and Becca Groves," Caleb said.

"Their brother married my sister," Paige answered.

"Such a small world," Col. Martin said. "Come on in. My wife is eager to see you again."

Caleb guided Paige into the house with his hand at the small of her back. She concentrated on getting through the door without tripping. It amazed her how distracting something as simple as Caleb's warm hand on her could be. "Colonel Martin was the first counselor in the bishopric when Alisa and I were baptized. He and his wife took us under their wing that first year. I think they missed having their kids around, so we became family."

"Tom! Caleb!" A sweet voice came from the kitchen. A small woman rushed up to the Marines. She looked like she should sit on the stand with the General Relief Society Presidency. "You're finally here."

She pulled Tom into a tight hug. She turned and hugged Alisa. "Alisa! I'm so excited for you two. I'm so sorry we can't come to the wedding, but I'm glad we could see you before you set off on your new life together."

"It's a small wedding, anyway," Alisa said.

"Caleb." Sister Martin hugged him and rubbed his back. "It's so marvelous to see you again. And who's this?" She glanced over at Paige.

"This is Alisa's best friend, Paige Ellis," he answered.

"Oh!" she exclaimed. Her smile got bigger, and she hugged Paige. "We've heard so much about you. I'm so glad we finally get to meet you."

"Seems everyone's heard about me," Paige said, cheeks coloring. She glanced over at Caleb whose cheeks were a guilty shade of pink.

They introduced the Martins to Becca and Lucie. It was a polite but less enthusiastic greeting.

"So," Sister Martin said, clasping her hands together. "There's enough room if the sisters share a room. And I'm almost done with lunch. It's nothing fancy. Just things to put hoagies together. I hope you're hungry."

"Sister Martin, where's Henry?" Tom asked.

"He should get home any moment," she said. "He opted to do a summer semester, so he's not around a lot."

She ushered them all out to the yard. She had picnic tables with red-checkered tablecloths loaded with food—more than enough to feed everyone. Sister Martin's version of 'nothing fancy' included several types of salad, chips, sodas, fruit and veggie trays, and an array of desserts.

"You always go overboard, Sister Martin," Alisa said.

"I know, I know," she repeated, a wide grin on her face. "But I'd rather have too much than too little."

"I've missed you," Alisa said, giving the older woman another hug.

"And you, dear," Sister Martin replied. She studied Paige. "What do you do for a living?"

"I teach third grade in West Jordan," Paige replied. She peered over her shoulder and saw Caleb still stood behind her.

"Oh, what a wonderful age," she said.

"It's true. They are so cute, and most of them are still so eager to learn and please."

"And you're not married?"

"No. Still single," Paige answered.

"You're such a sweetheart. I'm sure the Lord has a special young man in mind for you." Sister Martin looked back at Caleb and winked at Paige. "Now, everyone, please take as much as you can eat. Then later tonight, George will fire up the barbeque."

The front door opened, and Paige turned around to discover a young man frozen at the threshold. He looked a little like a deer caught in headlights.

"Henry," Tom said, going over to the young man and giving him a bro hug. "I'm glad you could make it. We just got here. Everyone, this is Henry Benning. He went to the local branch with Caleb and me before he decided he'd rather get a college degree than hang out with us."

"Hi," he responded.

Tom made the introductions. After filling her plate, Paige looked around for a place to sit. Henry sat by himself at one of the picnic tables, mostly picking at his food. He kept glancing toward where Becca and Lucie were talking to Caleb and Tom.

"Do you mind if I sit down?" Paige asked.

"No, go ahead," he replied.

"You were in the Marines too?"

"Yeah. Did my four years and got out."

"So political science is your major. What's your plan?"

"I'm studying to be an analyst."

"That makes sense. Don't have to be in the spotlight when you're an analyst."

Henry gave her the first hint of a smile and nodded his head.

"I'm excited about tomorrow," Paige said. "It's been a really long time since I've been at a lake, let alone on a boat."

"Water should be comfortable," he replied. "It's too bad there'll be so many of us. It's an excellent time for fishing."

"Do you like the great outdoors?"

"One of the few places where I can breathe," he said.

"Logan and Cache Counties are good for that type of open country," Paige said, looking over at Becca and trying to hide a smile. "Good horse country."

"Definitely," Henry said.

Becca laughed again. Henry's eyes glanced over at her.

"So, what's the plan for tomorrow?" Paige asked.

"I was thinking we could head up to the lake at around 6 a.m. It'll get us on the lake before the holiday crowd shows up. Then there will be lots of time for swimming and skis."

"I'll bet with as much food as we have here, I could help your aunt put together a picnic lunch for the boat tomorrow."

He nodded and glanced over at Becca again. Paige looked over and noticed Caleb looking at her. Her heart leaped into her throat, and she gave him a slight smile. He returned it but turned back to the conversation.

"So, you knew Caleb from before?" Henry asked.

The question took Paige by surprise. "Uh, yeah, we dated in high school."

"That explains a lot."

Paige was about to ask what he meant by that when Tom approached Henry.

"Come on," Tom said, slapping Henry on the shoulder as he cradled a football with his other hand.

Henry followed Tom onto the open expanse of lawn. Becca and Lucie flanked the men like a mini group of cheerleaders. Paige turned so she could watch while still sitting at the picnic table. Alisa sat down with Paige.

"Now this should be fun," Alisa said with a smirk.

"I'm not complaining," Paige answered. "I'm pretty sure the whole point is to show off a little."

"For sure. But I love it."

"How's everything between you and Tom?"

"Fine. He seems a little more relaxed now that we're not at the house anymore."

"I can't believe in about a week you'll be a married woman."

"I know. I'm so excited and nervous at the same time."

Paige took her friend's hand in hers. "It will be great."

They sat and watched the ball being thrown around. At one point, Caleb jumped up to catch the ball, and his shirt flew up exposing a very fit torso. Paige found herself pondering the exact configuration and definition of his stomach muscles until she realized she'd been staring pretty hard. She turned her gaze away, her cheeks burning.

"What were you and Caleb talking about before we left for Logan?" Alisa asked.

"About things that have happened in the last forty-eight hours."

Alisa rolled her eyes. "Oh, is that all?"

"I guess. He wanted to make sure we're still friends."

"It's better than you two still fighting . . ."

"I think we're past that," Paige said, eyeing Caleb as he tackled Henry to the lawn. "Your wedding is the priority. The finish line is you happily off on your honeymoon, and we're on the last leg."

Paige sighed. She watched him and enjoyed the view. He smiled more when he played with his friends, and it was a beautiful sight to see. Seemed since he'd come back to Utah, he had smiled little. It was too bad. He had a magnificent smile, and the sight made her stomach do flip-flops. She wouldn't know what to do with herself if he ever directed the full strength of that smile at her again.

Chapter 18

With the onset of the evening, everyone had gathered in the Martins' living room. Everyone congregated on available furniture. Tom and Alisa sat snuggled up on the loveseat. Alisa lay against Tom's chest wrapped up in his arms looking as contented as Paige had ever seen her. Tom excitedly told stories of their time in South Carolina when Caleb and Alisa first joined the Church.

"So, I told Caleb he needed to tear the bread up into small pieces, and I would take care of the left side trays if he'd do the right side. The piano player is playing and playing and playing. I'm at the middle tray and Caleb's working on the first of his trays. Finally, I look over, and he's got bites the size of peas," Tom said. "I kid you not."

"I remember that," Alisa exclaimed. "Poor Caleb."

"Yeah, yeah," Caleb said. "I wanted to say the sacrament prayer right the first time. I was going to say it by memory, and I was nervous. I was repeating it in my head while I tore up the bread at the same time. I didn't realize what I'd done to the bread until Tom's over there elbowing me in my ribs."

"You did just fine," Sister Martin said, patting Caleb on the knee. "It's a lot of pressure those first few times."

"It's a terrible feeling to look over and there's the branch president shaking his head because you said it wrong," Caleb said, grinning at her.

"But he did it, and the branch president didn't have to shake his head," Tom said.

"And I tear slightly larger bread chunks now too," Caleb stated.

"It makes me so proud to see how much you've grown in the gospel, Caleb. And our beautiful Alisa getting married . . . Time does fly," Sister Martin said, getting up from her easy chair. "Well, I'm worn out, everyone. I think I'll head to bed now. Stay up as late as you like."

"I think I'll join you, my dear," Colonel Martin replied, pushing himself up as well. "I'll see everyone in the morning."

As soon as the older couple left, Lucie jumped up. "I want to play a game. How about we play Truth or Dare?"

Paige groaned. Alisa laughed. "What, Paige? Too chicken to play Truth or Dare?"

"I'm just having flashbacks of dares like Seven Minutes in Heaven from high school. Can we leave that one out?"

"Good idea. Let's also leave out anything you shouldn't do with an engaged person or you wouldn't do in front of Colonel and Sister Martin," Alisa said.

"Fine," Becca pouted. "But you're taking all the fun out of it."

"I think you'll live," Alisa insisted. "I'm going first. Paige, truth or dare?"

"I don't trust you, so of course you'd pick me," Paige said. "Truth."

"Paige, have you kissed Elliot yet?"

Paige laughed. "No, but I'm sure he wishes I had."

"I should have figured," Alisa said, rolling her eyes. "I'm making it harder next time."

"All right, my turn," Paige said, looking around the room. Henry appeared to be trying his best to be a part of the wall. A Cheshire grin spread across her face.

"Becca, truth or dare."

"Me?" Becca giggled. "Okay, um, dare!"

"Okay, I dare you to sit on Henry's lap for five minutes," Paige replied.

Caleb and Tom whooped. Henry had gone three shades of red.

"That one's easy," Becca said. She walked over to Henry and made herself comfortable on his lap. She draped her arm over his shoulders, totally unfazed by the dare.

Paige glanced over at Caleb. He grinned and shook his head.

"Want me to set a timer?" Caleb asked.

"No, I'll remember," Becca replied. "Okay, my turn. Hm, Caleb since you spoke up—truth or dare?"

"I hate this game," he said. "Let's see. Truth?"

"I love Truth! Let's see. What's the best kiss you've ever had, including when, where, and with whom?"

It was Caleb's turn to go three shades of red, and Paige was sure she knew why.

"I'd have to say it was after Senior Prom," Caleb said, looking at his hands. "Paige and I took a ride in one of those carriages downtown. That was a really good night."

Paige's heart fluttered at the memory. Caleb had surprised her when he pulled her away from the group they'd been with. It had already been a magical night with Caleb looking drool-worthy in his tux and every slow song seemed perfect for them. But then he led her by the hand outside the hotel, and took her to a carriage waiting for them. Snuggled in beside him, Paige didn't think she could be any happier at the time. Then he'd leaned over and given her one of the most mind-blowing kisses they'd ever had. He'd cupped her face with his hands and kissed her slowly but passionately until she could barely breathe. His kiss seemed to have more than the normal amount of emotion fueling his touch. The kiss was more magical because of it.

Caleb still had his head down. Apparently, he'd found the kiss just as magical as she had.

"Aww, that's so cute," Becca said. "I love those carriage rides. I always ask the driver if I can pet the horses."

Paige rolled her eyes internally.

Caleb looked up and around the room. "Tom, truth or dare?"

"Dare," he said.

"Okay, you and my sister go on the front porch and do Seven Minutes in Heaven out there," Caleb grinned.

"Cheater!" Becca said, popping up from Henry's lap. "You said not that one."

"They're engaged, and their wedding is next week," Caleb stated. "They're allowed."

Tom didn't waste time arguing. He pulled Alisa to her feet and headed out the front door.

Those in the room giggled. Becca sat down next to Caleb. "Since Tom isn't here to take his turn, I'm taking another one," Becca said. "Henry, truth or dare?"

Henry looked genuinely shocked she had picked him. "Uh, dare, I guess."

"Hmm, do you know the Texas two-step?"

Henry looked like a captured racoon. "Yes."

Becca clapped. "You can teach me. That's the dare. Teach me the Texas two-step and you get bonus points if you can show me how to spin. Lucie, what song was I listening to the other day? Oh, right! *Haywire*. I'll pull it up on my phone. Pull back the chairs. This will be fun!"

While they were busy, Paige stood up and walked out to the back porch. She needed some fresh air.

Chapter 19

Paige sat down on the rocking chair located on the back porch of the Martins' house. The twilight sky, with its brilliant pinks and oranges, slowly darkened into rich blues and purples. A crescent moon hung low as a dazzling contrast to the night sky, inviting the stars to twinkle around it. There was a peaceful quiet here, despite the hum of music and laughter from inside the house.

She leaned her head back against the chair. What Alisa said yesterday came back to her. Something's got to give. *Yes, it does,* she thought. And as much as she wished to declare bravely what was in her heart, she knew she couldn't. Looking at Caleb made her contemplate what had been. And then she considered what was possible, and her courage would buckle under the weight of it. She'd much rather spend the rest of her life wondering about the *what if* than have Caleb tell her directly to her face he'd lost any love and respect for her a long time ago. But not knowing was also killing her. Alisa and Elliot suggesting he did care for her still was killing her. She was sometimes sure they were right. Sometimes he was so sweet to her or funny, but then he'd turn around and be such a jerk. Then she wondered if all she'd seen was what she wanted to see in him.

The door to the back porch opened. She turned to see Caleb pull up a cooler next to her chair and sit down.

"Nice night," he said.

"Yes, it is." She nodded.

"Mind if I join you?" he asked.

"Not at all."

"Had enough of the noise?"

"I'm regretting we brought the noise with us."

Caleb chuckled. "Come on. You remember that age. Wasn't everything funnier and louder back then?"

"Maybe for you," she replied. "I don't remember being so . . . boisterous."

"I don't know," Caleb said, grinning. "The Paige I remember liked to laugh a lot."

She smiled at him. "I had someone back then who knew how to make me laugh."

"But not now?"

Paige looked away. "I guess I've grown up and am a bit more selective in what I find funny anymore."

Caleb laughed out loud. "Wait a minute. I seem to recall someone nearly getting us kicked out of the bakery yesterday and who found that completely hilarious."

Paige whipped her head back to him, her eyes narrowed. "Excuse me, but you started it. You got frosting all over my face!"

The absolutely unrepentant expression on his face both galled and delighted her.

"You're incorrigible," she said as she tried to restrain her grin.

He beamed back at her. He scanned the lawn in the twilight, seemingly content for the moment to just sit there in her company.

"I did come out here for a reason. Would you please grant me one small favor?"

"I guess it depends on what it is," she answered.

"Typical Paige answer," he grumbled. "Can I, without interruption, finish explaining my side about the whole Becca thing?"

Paige dropped her chin to her chest. She had nothing to lose hearing his side. It actually said something that he was insisting on explaining it.

"Yes," she replied after a minute.

"You're sure?" he responded.

"Yes," she repeated a bit more forcefully. Was he going to sit there and annoy her now that he had her undivided attention?

Caleb waited a moment, and then said, "Becca came over to talk to me, and while I was out there, she said something to me I couldn't hear. I should have seen it coming with her leaned against me like she was. When I bent over to ask her to repeat herself, she kissed me. I admit, I kissed her back just to see what it was like. She's a pretty girl. The problem is that while she's fun to hang out with, I'm not attracted to her like that. First, as you so persistently assert, she's too young for me. I prefer women closer to my own age. Maybe older women. I haven't tried that one yet. Second, it's hard to hold a conversation with someone when all they can talk about is country music, hair dye, and horses. Not that there's anything wrong with that but after a while . . . well . . . What you saw with Becca the other day meant nothing to me. Becca, I'm sure, kissed me because the opportunity presented itself." He paused as if he were waiting for her to say something. She gazed at him, letting what he said sink in. Alisa had been right about that.

After a few seconds of her silence he continued, "I also wanted to make certain you didn't misunderstand why I kissed you."

That made Paige sit up straighter in her chair, and bile come up into her throat. Here it was. He was planning on letting her down gently, right here in the middle of Logan where she'd have no place to go to process the rejection but in the room of a virtual stranger's home. At least Alisa was here, but again, Paige had promised her this week would be drama-free. Alisa was supposed to have the happiest day of her life in seven days. She didn't need to be consoling her best friend as she fell apart right before then.

"Which time?" Paige asked, nearly choking on the emotions she was forcing back down.

"Which time?" he faltered, pushed off-kilter by the unexpected question. "I was talking about the backyard—"

"Oh, right," she said abruptly. "You know, don't worry about it, Caleb. I understand. It meant nothing to you then either. It was a got-caught-up-in-a-moment thing."

"Was it that way for you?" he asked, surprised.

"What does it matter? Things would be better if they went back to the way they were."

"I'm not sure that's possible anymore," he said, inspecting her face. Her stomach fluttered. "Why would you want them to? Change isn't a bad thing, and the experiences make us grow."

"Like kissing girls a decade younger than you?" Paige mumbled.

"What was that?" Caleb said, leaning into Paige. "Did I hear the rumblings of jealousy over there, Paige Ellis?"

"No, Caleb Watson, you did not."

Caleb gave her a knowing look and chuckled as he got up from his cooler and walked down the porch steps onto the lawn.

"Knock it off, Caleb," she said.

"I didn't expect you'd become so stodgy in your old age."

"Stodgy?" she demanded, getting up off her chair and marching down the stairs to look him in the face. She poked him in his chest. "Forgive me if I don't throw my hair around and laugh like hyena whenever you say something clever."

He continued to smile at her until she folded her arms at him.

"Miss Ellis, I would never expect you to consider me funny or clever. You're insisting awfully hard you're not jealous, but every time I bring it up . . . phew! In fact, I don't recall you ever saying you believed me when I say I didn't ask for her to kiss me. That right there says you're jealous."

"Why would I be jealous of someone who has to trick people into kissing her? If I felt like kissing someone, I would. I would go up and give them a nice full kiss and everyone would be on the same page about it." Paige jerked her chin up in defiance of what Caleb insinuated.

"Really?" he said, taking a step forward, reducing the space between them. "That's not how it seemed the other night. In fact, if I recall correctly, I kissed you and you seemed more than happy to go along with it until I got slapped. Do you often change your mind mid-kiss?"

"And I seem to recall I already apologized for slapping you," Paige said.

"Still stung," he said, rubbing his cheek as if it was still smarting. "You could have avoided a lot of this if you'd admit to yourself that Becca kissing me made you feel just a bit jealous and you overreacted. That's all."

"The only thing I admitted to is overreacting. You wish I was jealous," she said, looking him up and down. She started back up the porch.

"Where are you going?" he demanded.

"Back in the house," she said, turning to face him. "I want to get up early tomorrow to help Sister Martin get the picnic together."

"No, you don't," he said, stepping forward and throwing her over his shoulder. The ease with which he picked her up sent her heart racing. "I'm not done with this conversation yet."

"Caleb!" she cried. "Put me down."

"Admit it. You were jealous," he responded.

From behind them came a hissing noise. When Paige looked up, the Martins' sprinkler system had come on.

"Don't you even think about it, Caleb!" she yelled, pounding on his back. She may as well have been pounding on a granite slab.

"You think I'm fooled by this cool act of yours? It hasn't changed in ten years," he said.

"I don't even know why it matters."

“Really?” He started walking toward the sprinklers. “I guess you do still need to cool off.”

“Caleb! I’m so serious right now. Put me down. If I get wet, bad things will happen.”

“I’m waiting.”

“Fine, it made me feel a little jealous. Geez.”

He put her back on her feet. She realized how very close they were when she peered up into his hazel eyes. His warm breath floated over her forehead as his soft eyes traveled down her face to her mouth. But then the image of Caleb kissing Becca popped into her head again. A sharp twisting assaulted Paige’s stomach. What she suspected were Caleb’s reasons for kissing her on the patio of her parents’ home still smarted, not to mention her utterly useless feelings for him. He was going home in a week. Kissing him would be so easy in this moment, but she couldn’t give him or herself the wrong idea. Sympathy kisses were bad enough. Exploring-what-might-have-been kisses were worse. She wouldn’t be that vulnerable with him again. Not with the wedding a week away. She slowly pushed herself back from him.

“What are you guys doing back here?” Tom asked, coming out onto the porch.

“Making sure Miss Ellis and I here have an understanding,” Caleb said, holding Paige’s arms as she held her hands against his chest. Tom smirked at his friend, shook his head and went back into the house.

“Goodnight, Caleb,” she said, letting go and turning out of his hands. She hurried back toward the house just in case he got any further ideas about sprinklers or kisses. “I’ll see you tomorrow morning.”

She turned her head to glance at him as she passed through the door. He stood in the same spot on the lawn, hands in his pockets. She took in a shuddering breath and closed the door.

Chapter 20

Paige wrapped sandwiches in the kitchen with Sister Martin early the next morning. The sun had just come up over the mountains intensifying the azure blue skies dotted with clouds. Perfect weather for boating on a lake. The older woman stood next to her, portioning out the fruit salad into Ziploc bags.

"It's going to be a gorgeous day," Paige said.

"I think you're right," Sister Martin replied. "Don't forget your sunscreen."

"Yes. I would hate to be all sunburned for Alisa's wedding photos," Paige replied. "I'm so excited for her and Tom. She deserves a good man."

"He is a good young man, and faithful too," Sister Martin said. "He had a rough upbringing, but he's kept close to the Lord. That's important. In life, but as a Marine as well."

"I'm sure."

Paige watched as Sister Martin expertly packed the cooler with the lunch items so there was no space wasted. She marveled at the woman's precision—all the sandwiches, drinks, and other sides were packed in for maximum efficiency.

"You have such a lovely home, Sister Martin," Paige said. "I hope to have one like it someday."

"Thank you, dear," she said, as she bustled around the baskets. "It's been over forty years in the making."

"How did you deal with moving around all the time?" Paige asked.

"You get very, remarkably good at keeping what's important and letting go of what isn't," she replied. "And you get very skilled at packing up boxes."

"I can imagine," Paige said, chuckling.

"You'll have your own system after a while," Sister Martin noted.

"I'm not in the military," Paige replied.

Sister Martin gave Paige a cheeky grin. Caleb walked into the kitchen. Paige gave him a shy smile.

"How are we doing in here, ladies?" he asked. "Do you need help getting anything packed?"

"No, no, Caleb," Sister Martin answered. "We're almost done here. Maybe you can take these to the trucks. Henry's outside getting the boat hitched."

"Good morning, Paige," Caleb said.

"Morning, Caleb," Paige said, trying to act normal.

"You two are so cute together it's a wonder you two still aren't married," Sister Martin said. Even Caleb's cheeks reddened. "I remember when George and I dated. It didn't take us very long to decide we wanted to be together. Once we got past all the stuff and nonsense of everyone's expectations for us, it was clear to see we were perfect for each other."

She patted each on the arm and shuffled out of the kitchen.

"Does she think we're secretly dating or something?" Paige asked. "She keeps giving me all these winks and knowing nods since I got here."

Caleb smiled. "Yeah, I've tried to tell her, but I don't think she believes me."

“She’s so sweet, though,” Paige said, picking up a cooler and a basket.

“That she is,” Caleb said, holding the door open for Paige. They made their way over to the truck with the boat attached. Henry stood in the truck's bed and took the cooler from Caleb.

“Morning, Henry,” Paige said.

“Morning, Paige,” he replied. “Caleb, I think we’ll have to pack the baskets in the other cars. I’ve got all the life vests and water toys stowed back here.

Caleb looked around. “It will be a tight squeeze then. We didn’t have much room to begin with.”

“Load everything up in the back of that car, and whoever was sitting there can ride with me.”

“Then that would be me,” Paige replied. “I hope you don’t mind.”

Henry probably preferred Becca. Then again, his shy awkwardness wouldn’t do their alone time any favors.

“No, you’re fine,” he said.

Paige carried the baskets over to her car and loaded the stuff in the backseat. Caleb approached her and leaned on the door.

“I can go with Henry, if you want.”

“I like Henry. He and I had a nice little chat yesterday,” Paige replied. “Besides, if it were a choice between Henry and going with the Lolly-twins, I’ll stick with Henry.”

“The Lolly-what?” Caleb asked.

“They’d want you to go with them anyway,” she said, patting Caleb on the cheek. A grimace spread across his face, and Paige walked away chuckling.

Soon everyone was packed in, and they were on their way up to the lake. Paige and Henry sat in companionable silence for the first little while. Paige had her feet up on the dash and was going through her phone.

"So, Paige, how do you know everybody? I know how you know Caleb and Alisa because they told me about you, but how do you know everyone else?"

Paige tried to hide a smile. "Tom and I only met a couple of weeks ago, though Alisa talked about him while they were dating. And Becca and Lucie are my brother-in-law's sisters."

"Brother-in-law?"

"Yes. Brent, their brother, married my sister."

"Oh, so you all know each other pretty well."

"You could say that."

"Is, uh, Becca dating anyone?"

"Not that I'm aware of. Her sister Lucie is waiting for a missionary to come home, but Becca's single."

He nodded his head.

"She's really friendly," Paige suggested. "You should try to talk to her."

"It's okay," he said, almost a mumble.

Paige didn't want to push him, though it was nice to have her suspicions confirmed. Perhaps there was a two-man water toy she could encourage them to go on together. *Not gonna lie. My motives are not entirely altruistic*, she thought with a sly smile to herself. The less attention she gave Caleb, the better.

"Can I ask you a question, Henry?"

"Shoot."

"What was Caleb like when you were in the Marines together?"

He glanced at her, and she could see the corner of his mouth tick up. "He was a good guy. Was pretty excited about joining the Church. A good Marine. And didn't date very much, if that's what you're after."

Paige turned red. She underestimated how savvy he was.

“Sort of. I was curious how different he was in the Marines from when I knew him.”

“You don’t stay a teenager for very long when you’re in combat.”

“I can only imagine. All I hoped for was that he was happy.”

Henry grinned. “That’s something I didn’t keep tabs on. Both he and Tom helped me through some hard times, and for that I’m grateful. I’d like to see him happy too.”

Paige gave Henry a slight smile. “You Marines never cease to amaze me. You guys come across all tough and hardened, but when it really comes right down to it, you really have each other’s backs.”

“Semper Fidelis—always faithful. To everything important in life, but particularly your brothers and sisters in the corps.”

“You’re an interesting guy, Henry. I’m glad we met.”

He flushed a bit. “That’s a first.”

“What?”

“Someone saying I’m interesting.”

“Maybe it’s because no one took the time to find out if you were or not.”

He shrugged. He didn’t look displeased with her compliment.

The lake came into view, and Henry turned off toward the docks.

They pulled up to the boat ramp at the lake. Henry positioned the truck so the boat and its trailer would back into the water.

Henry opened his door and stood up. "Let's load up all the food and stuff first. Then everyone get in before I back her up."

Everyone piled out of the cars and grabbed all the things they were bringing—baskets and coolers of food and drink, towels, and backpacks. The guys made quick work of loading the stuff in and then the girls climbed aboard.

"Hey, Tom, take the wheel on the boat? Back her up a little when I signal," Henry shouted.

Suddenly, Becca and Lucie erupted into cat calls. Paige turned around. Tom and Caleb had taken their shirts off so they were only in their swim trunks. The shirts ended up in the back of Henry's truck, and Caleb and Tom waded out to the boat and climbed aboard.

Tom took over the wheel on the boat and Henry got back into his truck and backed the boat into the water.

Paige found she could not help but stare as Caleb moved to sit down. It wasn't just that he was more fit than she expected, but that he had a huge tattoo that stretched across his upper back. Semper Fidelis. He turned around, catching her staring.

"What?"

She shook herself. "Nothing. Sorry. You got a tattoo?"

"Yeah, probably a couple years after I joined up. Is that a problem?"

"No. Just took me by surprise is all." It was yet another reminder that Caleb was not the teenager she used to know. "Can I see it?"

He turned around so she could examine his broad back. The *Semper Fidelis* was in a beautifully ornate font. Gorgeously rendered artwork of the Marine Corps anchor and globe sat between the words. Right below the globe and anchor was another Latin phrase and looked newer than the rest. She ran her finger across it.

"What does this mean? *Ex fide fortis.*"

"It means *from faith comes strength,*" he said, turning around. "I figured the Lord wouldn't mind one more tattoo if it represented my devotion to Him."

Paige nodded. "I love it. It's simple but profound."

"There was another one I liked, but I didn't want to have to explain all the details of what it meant constantly. *Alis aquilae—on eagle's wings.* It's a reference to Isaiah 40:31. Through faith in God comes strength to run and not be weary and walk and not faint. So *ex fide fortis* means nearly the same thing, but with less explanation."

"This might sound silly but all these years the dangers you face as a pilot was never a reality for me. I mean I understood what deployment could mean but it was like I took for granted that you'd be back after the time was up. Now, well . . . I know the Lord looks after all His children, but it makes me feel a little better that you'll take the Spirit with you into combat. It's an extra layer of protection."

He gave her a soft smile. "You do an awful lot of contemplating your mortality in a place like a combat zone. Before I joined the Church, I always felt like there was something missing. Like a step in a series of directions that made my place here on Earth more precarious than it should be. After Tom and I became friends, he'd talk to me about his experiences with prayer on his mission. I realized then what I was missing. There was a loving Heavenly Father that cared for me personally. I wasn't alone when I was in the air, and He wanted me to come home safe. I learned I could come to Him in prayer when things were hard and He'd be there. After my baptism, I realized something else pretty profound. The missing piece had been in front of me before. It was there while I was in high school, but I was too immature to see it."

Paige could feel tears threatening to well up in her eyes. She had to clear her throat before she could respond. "One more reason I have to be grateful you and Alisa have Tom."

Caleb going into war zones—the idea now filled her with a sense of dread. She'd gotten to know Caleb again—to see the man he'd become—and now it was a stark reality. She wondered how Alisa had done it all these years. She, of course, mentioned her nervousness to Paige when Caleb was deployed but even then, it was something Alisa seemed to take in stride overall.

Paige would worry about his safety and well-being even if they parted ways after the wedding and never saw each other again. Not merely because he was once someone she loved. He'd become someone she could respect. Besides, you didn't stop caring about a person because life had gotten in the way.

As he waded out to the boat, Henry said, "Let's go."

CHAPTER 21

Henry came aboard and took over the wheel as they made their way slowly toward the safety buoys. Paige inspected the lake. They were one of the first groups there. Finding a good spot for having fun would be easy having beat the crowds. Being a holiday weekend, the lake was sure to get busy as the holiday morning wore on. Bright sunlight streamed down from the sky, and only a slight breeze blew her hair around. The water lapped gently against the sides of the boat—perfect for skiing and kneeboarding. Paige hurried to braid her hair and secure it with a tie she had on her wrist. Once Henry punched the craft into high gear, she'd rather not have her hair all over the place.

The boat passed the line of buoys, and Henry pulled down on the gearshift. The vessel lurched forward as the motors roared to life. Becca and Lucie screamed, holding their hands in the air as the boat raced across the water. Even Paige enjoyed their enthusiasm. There was something about the wind whipping across your face and the boat slapping against the water as it rushed forward that made boating thrilling.

Paige glanced over at Alisa. Tom and she sat cuddled up together at the back of the craft, eyes only for each other. Paige smiled. Today was going to be a good day. Henry slowed the boat down once he got to an area in the lake where no other boats seemed to be. He threw a safety flag float into the water.

"Can we go swimming now?" Becca said, looking at Henry.

"Go ahead."

Becca and Lucie pulled off their pullovers, revealing cute swimsuits and their petite figures, before jumping into the water. Henry busied himself with the console of the boat, but Paige noticed his face flushed with color. She tried not to giggle. She took her own shorts off and pulled her t-shirt over her head. She searched around for a suitable place to stash her clothes when she saw Caleb staring at her. She was only wearing a simple blue one-piece, but she felt the weight of his stare.

"Coming in the water?" she said to him, trying to distract herself enough to keep all the blood from rushing into her face.

"Sure."

"Hey, lovebirds," Paige said to Tom and Alisa. "Don't forget we're here to have fun *in* the water."

Alisa stuck her tongue out at Paige. She couldn't blame her for wanting to be next to Tom. It was so close to their wedding day, and all the men, including Tom, looked healthy and fit with no shirts on.

"Coming, Henry?"

"Maybe I should stay with the boat."

"Tom's sitting right there. If there's a problem, I'm sure he can handle it."

"Yeah, come on, Henry," Caleb added. "Jump in. I'll be right after you."

Henry stood there for a minute, undecided. Becca screamed in delight on the side of the craft. He peered over. Paige motioned her head toward the water. He jumped in. Paige looked over at Caleb and smiled.

"Someone's got a crush," she said, leaning into Caleb.

"Henry and Becca?"

Paige nodded.

Caleb half-grinned and chuckled. "You're so evil. I wondered about that dare you gave Becca last night. Seriously, this is the first time I've ever seen him . . . I don't know what you would call it—willing to sort of put himself out there?"

"I think it's cute," Paige answered. "He was trying to act so cool on the way to the lake, but he asked me about her."

Caleb grinned. "Then good for him. I hope he comes out of his protective turtle shell for once. Shall we?" He pointed to the water.

Paige jumped up on the railing of the craft and did a perfect swan dive into the water. Caleb jumped in right next to her, cannonballing a wave of water into her face right as she was coming up for air.

"Jerk," she said, coughing and splashing him with water.

"Show-off," he said, splashing back.

"What?" she declared. "Just for that . . ." She leaned back in the water and kicked her legs as hard as she could. Caleb, with a wicked grin, averted his face while he swam toward her.

"Caleb, no, don't!" she exclaimed, as she tried to swim away, but he caught her around the waist. "Ah, no!"

He drove her under the water with both hands. She came up laughing. He tried swimming toward her again, and she quickly backstroked away. "Don't you touch me."

"I'd have to catch you first," he replied.

Becca and Lucie were trying not to drown between their peals of laughter. Even Henry had a grin on his face.

"Oh, yeah? You guys think that's funny, do you?" Caleb asked.

Caleb swam toward the girls. They screeched and swam away from him. Caleb nearly caught Becca, but she ducked behind Henry. Holding him by the shoulders, she yelled, "I'm protected by Henry now!"

Caleb gave Henry an appraising stare. Henry's face turned deepening shades of red as his smile spread across his face. Lucie still backed up and Caleb looked ready to pounce. He didn't see that Paige had come up behind him. She jumped on Caleb's back, wrapped her arms around his neck, and pulled him under the water.

Caleb came up with a smirk on his face. He started swimming toward Paige when a huge splash of water got him directly in the face.

Becca's donkey laugh erupted from the side. "Got you!"

"Oh, yeah?" Caleb asked, then suddenly changed directions and swam with surprising speed toward the petite blonde. She had floated away from Henry and hurried to swim back to him. Caleb splashed some water toward her, trying to get her in the face.

"No, you don't," Henry said, suddenly charging Caleb and tackling him in the water. The two men went under for a second.

"Hey, what the heck?" Caleb said once he surfaced. "Same team, bro."

"Right, bro. Remember that church basketball game and the *accidental* hip check?" Henry asked as he held him in a choke hold.

"That was totally innocent," Caleb said, even though he couldn't keep the edge of laughter out of his voice. "Can't blame a guy for trying to get set up for a three-pointer with certain bulky cowboys in the way."

"Come on, Henry, get him," Becca crowed.

Caleb arched himself backward, giving Paige and everyone else a delightful view of his abs before going under the water like a cresting dolphin. He popped back up, splashing the surfacing Henry in the face with his strong strokes. Now that Caleb was free of Henry, he tried swimming toward Becca again.

The two sisters started screaming and laughing, pushing water in front of them to keep Caleb at bay.

Caleb was woefully outnumbered in this fight, which made the game that much more funny. Paige swam as stealthily over to Lucie as she could. Becca turned her head and caught Paige coming up behind them.

"Lucie, look out!" Becca screamed.

Paige swam under the water and grabbed Lucie's leg before she noticed and yanked her under.

"I'll teach you to drown my sister!" Becca exclaimed.

Paige tried to splash Becca with a kick from her leg, but Becca was gaining on her. Just before Becca caught up, Paige ran into a warm body. She turned around into the smiling face of Caleb.

"She's almost got me," Paige laughed. Caleb pushed Henry away and grabbed Becca around the waist, pulling her away from Paige. Henry, seeing Caleb with his arm around Becca, jumped on Caleb. Paige let out a feral yell and jumped on Henry's back, trying to dislodge him from Caleb.

"What are you guys doing down there?" Paige heard Alisa yell.

"We're having fun," Caleb yelled back. "Go back to making out!"

Having Paige on his back was enough to distract Henry from Caleb, but Becca took advantage of Paige's distraction and charged her.

"Hah!" Becca yelled. Paige spun away from Henry and caught Becca by the waist and then pushed her under the water. Paige glanced over as Caleb shoved Henry under at almost the same time. They looked at each other and laughed. Paige swam up to Caleb and held her hands up for a double high five.

"Yeah!" Paige whooped as Caleb pulled her in for a hug.

"Good job, babe," he said into her ear. Caleb's term of endearment slapped her upside the head and dazed her. They were body to body in the water and the exertion from the water fight had them both heaving breaths right into each other's faces. Suddenly, she seemed too hot and lightheaded. She pulled herself out of Caleb's hold and swam to the boat just as Alisa and Tom were jumping in. Shaking, she pulled herself up the ladder and sat herself down on the nearest seat.

Her head was a mess. Too much had been happening too soon, and they had clearly defined none of it. It was always feelings and hints and moments. What was going on between them? She knew what she felt, but she'd been too chicken to say it when Caleb gave her the chance before they left for Logan. Her heart beat too quickly as she gulped in air. Now Caleb was calling her "babe" like he did back in high school. The term of endearment felt like a knife to the gut. Partly because she was too afraid to find out if that really meant he still cared for her. Partly because even if he did, he'd be leaving in six days. Then where would she be? Get him back for a few wonderful days only to have to send him away again. Except for this time, she'd have to watch him leave. Where was the fairness for either of them in that?

The boat's back end dipped a bit as Caleb climbed aboard and came up and sat next to her.

"I'm sorry, Paige," he said, trying to hug her to him. "It sort of slipped out."

"I know, Caleb," she responded. "It took me by surprise is all."

"Paige, we really need to talk," he said. "I thought if I could come here and get through Alisa's wedding—"

"Caleb, it's okay. You don't have to explain yourself."

"But what I'm trying to say is—"

"It doesn't matter."

He growled. "Would you let me finish a freaking sentence, please?"

She glanced at him, contrite.

"This is the crap I don't miss," he declared, standing up and putting his hands on his hips. "All I wanted to do was get through the wedding. I didn't want to revisit the past. But somehow, no matter how long it's been or who we're with, I'm reliving it with you, except this time I have no idea what's going on. And every time I've tried to ask you about it, you shut me down."

"Why say anything if it's going to cause a fight like it always seems to?" Paige asked, tears glistening in her eyes.

"Paige, you assume you know what I'm going to say before I can say a syllable. I haven't been able to get a word in edgewise since I got here. You have no idea how I feel about anything because you never ask."

"I'm sorry, Caleb," Paige replied. "I'm sorry if it ever seemed like I didn't care about your feelings. I care."

"Then give me a chance to talk uninterrupted for one minute. Give me at least that long to finish a thought. It was sort of cute when we were in high school. Now it's just annoying."

Paige's eyes narrowed. "Annoying? I'm so glad I understand how seriously you take me. If this is your version of getting a word in edgewise, then we might as well quit while we're ahead."

"Oh, my . . ." Caleb growled, throwing his hands up. "So that's it? Paige has decided the conversation's over, so it is?"

"You really expect me to talk to you when you just insulted me? You're a pretty brave man. Why would I allow you to talk to me like that when I don't allow anyone else to? Go back in the water. All you're going to do is piss me off more."

Caleb laughed a cold, unamused chuckle. "That's hilarious, Paige. All I wanted to do was enjoy time hanging out with friends Alisa and I hadn't seen in a long time. Instead, I'm walking around on eggshells, making sure I don't piss you off. I've been fielding your anger and jealousy all week. I can't relax for one minute because I wonder what I'm going to do wrong next. But I guess that shouldn't surprise me. There's been no time in my life when we've been together where you let me go unpunished. Why would I expect anything different now?"

"Why would I want to hang out with you, Caleb?" Paige asked, standing up herself. "When you walked off the plane, you acted like my presence offended you. And then you took every opportunity to reinforce the fact by rubbing it in my face that you'd rather be with Tweedledee and Tweedledum. My head swims with how fast you answered their beck and call. Every other minute you were gone off somewhere with them. So, I'm sorry if I didn't run around chasing after you trying to get you to pay attention to me!"

"You barely allowed yourself time to hang out with me, let alone get my attention. You expressed no interest in being around me unless it had to do with the wedding. Yet, those two girls expressed enough interest to include me in what they've been doing. So, when I had the chance to do something fun with people who actually want my company, what do you expect I'm going to do?"

"I expect you to get over yourself. But if that's too much to ask for, then by all means, hang out with those people less annoying than me. It's not like you care if I care or not. I've had to put up with so much crap since you got back, it will be a relief when you go home.

"I wanted Alisa to have a beautiful, stress-free wedding, but the only thing I've done is stress her out because I tried getting through to you. I did the wrong thing, or not enough, according to you, when I struggled to make amends for the past. I was inadequate, it seemed, when I apologized for graduation night. You didn't even have the courtesy of responding."

"What did you expect me to say?"

"I don't know. Something. Anything that said you understood what I was saying, even if you didn't want to forgive me. Apparently, I'm only deserving of being treated like the crap person you think I am. Do you know how awful I've felt for the last ten years, Caleb? Do you know how much it ripped my heart out to watch you walk away with the ring still in your hand that night? And I hoped you would have understood when I tried to explain it the other night. But obviously, I did a crappy job of explaining that too."

Tears sprouted from her eyes. She quickly covered her face in her hands and a few sobs escaped her throat. She could feel Caleb's hands on her arms. When she glanced up at him, he looked shocked and irritated.

"Paige, I don't know—"

Paige's anger bubbled up again. Why say anything if it was going to make her mad? Why open his mouth when whatever he was trying to say sounded so patronizing?

"Just don't," she hissed, pushing him away. "I've been speaking into the wind as usual. You'll always throw it in my face how wrong I was. I had hoped we could be friends. That's fine. You've obviously made your choice. Do me a favor? Tell everyone it's time for lunch. Maybe I'll have Henry get out the kneeboards or something for this afternoon."

"Doing it again. I'm sick of this," he gritted his teeth. "Fine. Believe whatever you want. This is pointless."

He jumped off the edge of the boat. Paige sunk down into the nearest seat and cried quietly to herself. Why did he insist on being such a jerk? She tried to do the right thing even though it was hard. Instead, he threw it back in her face. So apparently her apology had meant nothing. Awesome.

Paige got the plates and utensils out. She reminded herself that there were only six more days before the wedding. Caleb would be on a plane heading back to South Carolina to do whatever kept him busy. And then she'd start getting ready for the new school year and move on. Not with Elliot, though. These tumultuous feelings she had for Caleb only highlighted how very little attraction she had for the poor lawyer. He deserved to find someone who was as crazy about him as he was about her. But that wasn't Paige.

Soon after, everyone started piling back into the boat. Paige sat in the seat next to the captain's chair—as far away from Caleb as she could get without sitting on the bow of the ship. She glanced over at him occasionally, and she caught him doing the same. She helped hand out lunch and sat and ate, lost in her thoughts. Alisa came up and sat in the captain's chair across from her.

"Was I imagining things, or did I hear you and Caleb arguing?"

"Yup. Seems that no matter what I've tried to do, he's not interested in truces or apologies."

"What did he say?"

"Oh, accused me of being jealous and ignoring him," Paige replied. "Not sure how I can ignore him when he's never around."

"I don't know," Alisa said, rubbing her friend's arm. "I hoped you two would work it out."

"Lise, I'm sorry. I tried and all I can say is that it won't be me that starts anything from here on out," Paige sighed. "I've already promised you this is your special week. It won't be something we'll resolve this time. That doesn't matter because I'm going to make sure you're happy and sent off to your honeymoon in wedded bliss. That's the sole thing I will concentrate on."

Alisa nodded. "Even though it is my week, that doesn't mean I'm not allowed to worry about either of you."

"I know," Paige said. "You're going to have the most amazing day ever. I promise."

"The only way you could ruin my day is if you didn't show up," she said, hugging Paige.

"Not going to happen," Paige said, hugging her back. "Wild horses couldn't drag me away."

CHAPTER 22

"Come on, Paige!" Alisa shouted. "You can do it! I believe in you."

"Let me concentrate!" Paige yelled back. Sit back, knees up, tip of the board above the water, lean back when the boat moves forward and hold on. Paige thought each step of the instructions to herself. She would do it this time. She had to because she was tired of getting slammed in the face with water every time she toppled.

Paige held onto the tether, trying to keep her body upright and the tip of the kneeboard above the water. "Ok!"

Henry threw the boat into high gear. She closed her eyes and held on for dear life when she felt the tether go taut. The next thing she knew, she was skimming across the water. She screamed in delight. For a few fabulous seconds, she could feel the water rushing beneath the board and the wind whipping her face. That is, until she leaned a little to the left. Water rushed up her nose as she crashed to a stop. She pounded the water with her fists when she broke the surface.

Henry swung the boat around. "Do you want to try again?" he asked, amusement twinkling in his eyes when he came up alongside her.

"No, I'm done with this craziness," she said, handing the kneeboard up to the boat. Caleb grabbed it from her and helped her in. He wore a lifejacket and yelled, "My turn!" before jumping into the water.

"I can't wait to see him get water up his nose," Paige said to Alisa.

"Don't count on it," Alisa said. "Guys at the base spend a lot of time in the water."

Henry straightened the boat and tether line out. Once Caleb set himself up, he yelled, "Hit it!"

Henry propelled the boat forward, and for a second Caleb disappeared beneath the water. Cresting over the wake, he popped up and landed effortlessly. Paige folded her arms, trying not to smile. Caleb made kneeboarding look so easy the way he slid across the water. He steered himself toward a wake and flew into the air. Water splashed out behind him as he landed, completing a perfect aerial 360 on the opposite side of the boat's wake. Everyone in the boat cheered.

Caleb jumped back toward the middle to veer toward the right end of the boat. His board swung in a wide arc, cruising nearly parallel to the boat. With a slight adjustment of his body, he sent the board careening back toward the rear of the boat. He hit the wake at such a high-speed Paige squinted her eyes. The air he gained from hitting the wake at that speed was impressive. He sailed over both wakes and landed on the outside of the opposite wake, completely bypassing the middle. She took in a deep breath, realizing he'd made the jump, even with a little flair. He put his arm up in the air and whooped out a rebel yell. One more 360 got him back to the middle, and he let go of the tether. Henry swung the boat around to grab him.

"That was so awesome!" Becca said.

"You've been practicing with Riley, haven't you?" Tom nudged Caleb.

"And you call me a show-off," Paige said, shaking her head.

"It's called skills," he said, a mischievous glint in his eyes. He plopped himself down on the nearest seat.

"Anyone else want to try it?" Henry said, glancing at Becca.

"I want to jump in the water. It's getting so hot!" she stated. Henry put the safety flag in the water. Becca scrambled up on the edge. "Lucie, I bet you I could do a flip off the side. Watch."

Becca jumped, rolling forward in a perfect spin into the water. "Try it," Becca yelled at her sister.

"No," Lucie said. "I'm jumping in. Watch out." Lucie daintily jumped into the water.

"I am pooped," Caleb said. "Knee boarding's fun, but man if it doesn't wear you out."

"Getting old, son," Tom said, kicking his friend.

"Must be," he said, stretching, all the muscles of his chest and torso flexing in a mesmerizing way. Paige had to keep from staring.

Becca climbed the ladder. "I'm doing a reverse now."

"Do you think that's a good idea?" Paige asked.

"I'm fine," Becca said, giving Paige a sour look. "I used to do them all the time on the diving team."

"Yeah, but the side of the boat's not a diving board," Caleb said.

"Just watch," she retorted.

She flexed up on the balls of her feet and raised her arms above her head. Before she could jump, another boat's wake made the boat rock a little, but Becca steadied herself and got into position again. She crouched down low and bounced once and then, with a powerful leap, lifted off the side.

She leapt up and as far away from the boat as she could. Her body jackknifed before she stretched back and splashed into the water. Paige only realized a second later that she'd been holding her breath and her chest.

Becca came back up the ladder. "Ah, such a rush! One more time. I forgot how fun those are."

"Becca . . ." Paige tried to say.

Becca got back up on the side of the craft. Once again, she positioned herself on the side of the boat, her face beaming and wet. She ignored Paige, though Paige had stood up and so had Caleb and Henry. She crouched a little and pushed off. A soft sound of wet skin rubbing against plastic could be heard right before Becca made an awkward jump off the boat. She jackknifed and leaned back, but she was not far enough away from the boat. Her head smacked the hull with a sickening thud and she splashed down hard into the water. Lucie screamed. Those who hadn't already stood up were on their feet in a second. Henry jumped first into the water. Paige and Caleb rushed to the side where she had disappeared,

"Help me get her up!" Henry yelled.

Tom stood beside Caleb and helped him pull a half-conscious and bleeding Becca out of the water. Paige searched for the first aid kit. Ripping it open, she pulled out some pads and gauze.

"Turn her over carefully," Tom said. "Let's see how bad it is."

The wound was deep and bleeding everywhere. Paige handed the pad and gauze to Caleb, and he carefully put pressure on the wound and wrapped the gauze around her head. "This isn't enough. Do we have a towel or something?"

Paige looked around and found her towel and handed it to Caleb. "Thanks," he said, looking up at her. She nodded. She watched as Caleb and Tom expertly wrapped Becca's head in the towel to stem further bleeding. With a few other towels, they wrapped her up like a burrito in case she went into shock.

A crying Lucie climbed the ladder with Henry right behind her. Alisa sat Lucie down next to her and held her around her shoulders while she cried.

Becca's head lolled as they turned her over onto her back. "What are we doing?" she asked, her words slurring almost as if she were drunk.

Henry kicked the boat in gear and sped to the docks.

Paige held her hand to her mouth. Stupid girl. Poor stupid girl. But what could Paige have done? You can't get someone to listen to reason if they don't want to hear it. Paige squatted down next to Becca and Caleb.

"We need to get her to a hospital," Paige said.

"Yeah, Tom and I will take her while Henry gets the boat packed up," Caleb said.

"Wait, have you ever been to Logan?" Paige asked.

"Maybe once," Caleb said.

"Have Henry take her. He'll know exactly where the hospital is. We'll take care of the boat and get it to the Martins. He can take my car."

Paige looked over at Henry. His solemn face glanced over at her and nodded. They made good time over the open water. Still, it seemed to take forever to make it back to the dock once past the safety buoys. Tom and Caleb jumped out of the boat and waited for Henry to lower a still semi-conscious Becca down to them.

"Tom, do you still have my keys?"

"Alisa, find the keys in my bag," he exclaimed as he and Caleb carried Becca to the car. Alisa threw the keys at Henry.

He was getting off the boat when Lucie cried, "Wait! I have to go with you. I can't leave her. She needs me."

"Let's go," Henry said. Lucie scrambled to follow him off the boat.

Alisa looked around at the blood spattered everywhere. Her chest heaved trying to keep control of herself. Paige went over to her and hugged her. "She'll be okay. It's a good sign she was conscious when they left."

"Stupid girl," Alisa said. "What was she thinking?"

"How about we find a bucket and start cleaning out the boat?"

Alisa nodded, but she still looked angry and scared. By the time Tom and Caleb got back, the boat had most of the blood cleaned out. As soon as Alisa saw her fiancé, she dissolved into tears.

Tom took her in his arms and rubbed her back. "It's okay. She'll be okay."

Caleb looked at Paige. "Are you all right?"

"Other than being shook up a bit, I'm fine."

"You warned her. And look what happened," he said, almost a growl. "Idiotic."

"I can't disagree with you," she replied. "I hope she'll be okay."

His face softened. "So do I. Let's get this boat back to the Martins."

CHAPTER 23

After a bit of trial and error, they got the boat back up on the trailer without damaging it. Tom and Alisa were taking the Watsons' car, so that meant Paige was going with Caleb. She was a little peeved at him still, but he was better company than a virtually married couple.

Paige had her feet back up on the dash as she looked out the window, watching the forests pass by.

"I hope you don't get mad at me for saying this," Caleb said. "But you really impressed me back there. I didn't realize you could be so cool and collected in an emergency."

Paige shrugged. "I didn't see a need to panic when we needed to help Becca."

"It was genius when you suggested Henry take her," he said. "If I didn't know any better, I'd say you had an ulterior motive."

Paige gave him a sad smile. "I didn't. It made more sense than you and Tom driving all over Logan. But let's just call it a fringe benefit for Henry."

Caleb chuckled softly. "Definitely."

They sat in silence after that. She continued to stare out the window, but her thoughts were on the Marine sitting next to her. Ten years had changed so much for both of them. Caleb had grown in height and stature. He'd accomplished a number of the goals he'd set for himself while he was still in high school. Few their age could brag the same. As irritated as she'd gotten with him earlier, she couldn't deny that was something that made her particularly proud of him. But he had a way of setting her temper off like no one else could. He'd crawled under her skin more than once; that made her want to send him off to South Carolina at the first possible moment.

Yet, it still bothered her that nothing seemed to have been resolved between them. Maybe that was why she'd been so touchy with him lately. She really wanted to know he'd heard her apology and understood it. She wanted to make sure that he left Utah knowing she broke her own heart right along with his that night. Paige rubbed her legs and stifled a sob that threatened to bubble up from her throat. No matter how irritated she was with him, the silence in the cab was killing her. She peered over at him.

"Will you be in the sealing room when Tom and Lise get married?" she asked.

"Yes," he replied. "Went through the temple a couple of years ago."

"I didn't want to assume, and Lise hadn't mentioned it that I can remember," Paige said. "Lots of guys wear undershirts."

"Yes, I'll be there," he said. He glanced over at Paige. "I can't imagine Lise never talked to you about me. Sometimes it seems like you know hardly anything at all about me."

Paige smiled dimly at him. "It was on purpose—a sort of understanding between us. You were like Fight Club. We didn't talk about you—much. Not because I wasn't curious. I figured it would be better the less I knew." *It would hurt less*, Paige thought, *especially if you had married someone else.*

Caleb chuckled. "Fight Club. That's funny."

Paige couldn't laugh with him. The wedding was days away, and Caleb was leaving for South Carolina after that. Who knew if they'd ever see each other again. The thought depressed her. She picked at her fingernails, not sure what to say.

"I can tell something's bothering you," he stated. "If this is about what we said earlier, I wish it hadn't ended in a fight."

"If you want the truth, my head's a mess," she replied. "Our fight earlier didn't help, but it's more than that. We have our differences and our history, but I don't want you to go home still mad. I don't want us to have any regrets, and I'd regret it if you left and still resented me."

"Paige, I don't . . ." He scratched the back of his head and grimaced. "I don't resent you. But I was angry. I was more than angry—hurt, heartbroken, confused. You weren't making any sense that night. I was so sure you would say yes, but you were giving me all these reasons you were saying no.

"It's funny how hindsight makes everything a lot clearer. That clarity became even more crystal the more the missionaries discussed temples and forever families. I finally grasped what you were trying to say. I wanted to tell you. I should have told you."

He glanced over at her, pain and guilt in his eyes.

"The thought of that night still made me angry, and I couldn't bring myself to tell you. The missionaries explained it so well, it was almost like you'd explained it wrong on purpose or something. So that didn't help anything. But having to explain it to my parents for Alisa and Tom's wedding, I realized how difficult that was. I realized how really hard explaining all that is without them having the context for it.

"I'm not angry anymore, and I don't want you to feel guilty anymore. I forgive you for everything in the past, if you forgive me for being too prideful to tell you I finally understood you."

"I forgive you." Tears dripped down Paige's cheeks. "Thank you, Caleb. You don't understand how much that means to me—to know."

He grabbed her hand and laced his fingers through hers. Enjoying the warmth of his hand in hers only made what she was feeling deeper and more poignant. Dripping tears turned to silent sobs. He held her hand as she cried. She'd gained some composure by the time they pulled up to the Martins' storage shed.

"Doing okay?" he asked, turning to study her.

She nodded. He reached his hand up to her face, and with his thumb wiped away a tear that lingered on her cheek. She looked into his gorgeous hazel eyes.

"Paige, I want you to know I care about you," he said. "Whatever happens, I don't want you to doubt that for a second."

"I'd hoped," she responded. "I was pretty sure it was there under the anger. It's the same way I felt. I only wanted wonderful things for you in your life, and watching what I've seen of your career, I couldn't be more proud of you."

"That means a lot," he replied. "It means a lot because that's what I plan on doing until I'm old and crotchety. Life in the Marine Corps isn't easy. But to me, it's worth it. It's given me a sense of purpose and pride in myself. Then you add in all the things I've learned about the Plan of Happiness—it all fits together for me."

Paige smiled at him. "What happened to that goofy, good-looking kid who never took anything too seriously?"

"He's still in here. He's just grown up a lot."

She searched his eyes. "There's no doubt about that." Someone tapped at the truck window. Sister Martin stood waving at them.

"Okay, you two, what is going on? Why are you driving Henry's truck?"

They got out of the pickup and walked Sister Martin to the house, telling her about the day's events. Caleb opened the door for the two women as they entered the kitchen.

"Once I get the trailer unhitched, we should stop by the hospital so we can determine how Becca's doing and swap cars," Caleb said, as Paige finished. A smirk spread across his face. "Plus, as disappointed as Becca or Lucie may be, I'm sure Henry would like to have a shirt to wear. He ran off so quickly he forgot to get it out of the truck."

"You let me know if there's anything I can do," Sister Martin said. "Poor dear. I hope she's all right. I should talk to Henry about keeping her here one more night so she can rest."

"I'm sure Henry would love that," Paige replied.

Sister Martin winked and said, "Let me get a fresh change of clothes from Henry's room, and you can take that with you."

She left the room. Caleb and Paige turned to each other.

"Oh, no," he said.

"What?"

He ran a finger along the bridge of her nose.

Paige gasped. "Seriously?" She got her phone out of her pocket. Sure enough, the start of a nice pink sunburn spread across her nose and tops of her cheeks. "Of course I'd get fried only days away from the wedding! Stupid, pasty, white skin."

She removed her t-shirt and turned around so Caleb could inspect her back. "Please tell me it's not bad."

"Um," was all he said.

"Great. So I'll be pink and itchy for the wedding."

Sister Martin handed Paige a bag with Henry's clothes in it. "Oh, my. That's a nice sunburn you've got there."

Paige sighed.

"I have some aloe vera gel in my bathroom," she said. "You can put that on the burn, and it'll help keep you from getting too flaky. Help heal it up faster."

"But not fast enough for poor Lise's group photos," she said.

"It's not that bad," Caleb said, holding her chin and inspecting her face. "You could make it look like you're blushing, with a little extra powder."

Paige grinned at him. "Thanks."

Sis. Martin handed Paige the bottle of gel. The cool gel eased the tightness of the burn on her nose. She turned to Caleb. "Would you mind putting it on anywhere on my back that's red?"

She turned around and hissed the first time he applied the cold gel on her back.

"I'm sorry. Did I hurt you?"

"No. Not you—the stupid sunburn."

"I'll try to be as gentle as possible."

He rubbed more gel on the burn. It was pleasant, but not as pleasant as the warmth that radiated from Caleb's careful hand. She relaxed into his touch.

"That should do it," he announced.

"Thanks, I was thinking . . ."

Sounds of arguing came from the front yard. Paige and Caleb rushed to the front door.

"What are you talking about?" Alisa was screaming. "Do I even know you at all?"

"You took what I said wrong," Tom said.

"I'm not sure how I can misconstrue suggesting we live together first," Alisa retorted.

Paige's breath caught in her throat. Alisa and Tom turned to see Caleb and Paige standing in the doorway. Tom stomped off, and Alisa crumpled into a pile of tears.

Caleb jogged after Tom, and Paige rushed to hug Alisa. She cried so hard she was hiccupping. Paige sat on the ground, holding her. Alisa gained control before she whimpered, "What am I going to do? What is he even talking about?"

"He asked you to live with him first?" Paige asked.

"He gets a phone call from his dad telling him he's flying in town for the wedding. Then, the next thing I hear, they're arguing about when and where his mom is going to be staying. Then Tom gets off the phone and starts saying stuff like the wedding is crap. That we couldn't possibly know each other well enough for it to be eternal. Then he went off about how he'd rather live together for a while, get married at a justice of the peace, and then get sealed later." Fresh tears dripped down her cheeks. "Paige, that's not the way it's supposed to be, right? Did I miss something in Sunday School?"

"No, Lise. There's nothing wrong with getting married civilly, but if you could have eternity right off the bat, why wouldn't you? Nothing about marriage is guaranteed, but living together won't guarantee anything either. Sounds like his fears are getting the best of him."

"I hate his parents. This is them talking. This is their example," Alisa said. "They hate each other, and they fight all the time. But they got married in the temple first. So now Tom thinks that any old way is good enough? He should know better, right?"

"He should, but you've both been under a lot of stress lately. As crazy as he is for you, I can't imagine he's serious, Lise. Plus, you two aren't his parents. They made their own choices, but I'm sure they didn't start off feeling that way about each other. You don't marry someone you hate. Maybe you guys need a cooling-off period."

"I can't leave him, Paige," Alisa said. "I love him too much, but getting married civilly isn't what we talked about. That's not what we've been planning this whole time."

"I wasn't suggesting you should break up," Paige said. "I meant you have to talk to each other when you both aren't so angry. You can't give up on what you want, and Tom should respect that. I have hope for you guys. He probably needs time to think about what he said."

"He seemed to know exactly what he was talking about a few minutes ago," she declared.

"I'm willing to bet he was just thinking aloud, and sometimes things don't come out how they're meant. How about you help me pack up everything in the cars so we can leave?" Paige asked. "We'll stop by the hospital first to see how Becca's doing and then head home."

"Paige, I don't want to ride in the same car as Tom right now. I'm too angry, and I'm afraid we'll start arguing again."

"How about this? You go with Caleb in your mom and dad's car. It will give you a chance to talk to your twin. You need that time. I'll take Tom with me."

"You are the best friend ever, Paige," Alisa said, hugging Paige tightly.

"Not nearly as great as my best friend," Paige replied. Paige got up and pulled Alisa up after her.

CHAPTER 24

After Paige explained the plan to the Martins, Paige and Caleb headed to the hospital. Caleb, Paige, and Alisa shuffled into a tiny room. Tom opted to stay out in the hallway. Becca looked pale, but more alert. She had a huge bandage on her head. Lucie was curled up on a chair, fast asleep.

Paige gave Henry the bag. "Courtesy of your aunt."

"Oh, thanks. I was thinking it was getting a little cold in here," he said, grinning. He ducked into the room's bathroom. Becca's eyes followed him to the bathroom and only turned to everyone else when the door shut.

"Fifty stitches, can you believe it?" she asked. "Fifty. It took forever. Thankfully, if I get a scar, no one will see it unless I shave my head."

"You're looking a lot better, that's for sure," Paige replied. "What about a concussion?"

"A minor one," she said. "Once my mom and dad get here, they'll probably let me go home."

Henry came out of the bathroom wearing a Logan High FFA t-shirt and a pair of tight Wranglers. "My aunt must have really dug into my closet. I haven't worn this t-shirt in forever."

"I wish my high school had an FFA," Becca said, looking Henry over with a smile of appreciation. "I love country stuff. Of course, I don't have any horses, and we're not farmers."

"It's not all about rodeos and growing stuff," Henry said.

"Really? That's what the websites looked like," she replied.

"I'll tell you about it later," he said, giving her a wink.

Caleb, Alisa, and Paige all shared a knowing look. As soon as they did, all of them got amused smiles on their faces.

"I'll tell you guys. Henry was so sweet the entire time. I was such a crybaby when they put in the IV. He held my hand the whole time and told me to talk to him so I wouldn't be looking when they did."

"You weren't that bad."

"Yes, I was," she said, blushing a little but her mouth curved into a smile. "But thanks to you, it was better."

He smiled back shyly.

"We can take Lucie home if you want us to," Paige suggested.

"Nah, she was so tired after everything, she needs the rest," Becca said, glancing at her sleeping sister. "Mom and Dad shouldn't be too much longer, and we'll go with them."

"Becca, you and your parents should stop by the Martins' before you go home," Paige said. "Sister Martin is worried about you. She suggested you could stay an extra day if you're not up for the ride home." Paige gave Henry a slight smile.

"Sister Martin is so cute," Becca said. "I'll talk to my parents. Staying an extra day wouldn't be such a bad idea."

"It was great to hang out with you, Henry," Paige said, giving him a brief hug. "Take care of Becca, will you?"

“I’m doing my best, but she’s an easy patient to take care of,” Henry said, glancing down at the girl in the bed. “And I’m glad I got to meet you, too, Paige.”

“Who knows? Maybe our paths will cross again in the future.”

He nodded, but he couldn’t entirely hide the smile on his lips. Alisa and Caleb said their goodbyes, and they left to go back to the cars.

“I’m going home with Caleb. Paige will take you in her car,” Alisa said, before getting in the car and slamming the door. Tom sighed.

“I guess we’ll see you at the house,” Caleb said. Caleb looked concerned but smiled at Paige. She smiled back before turning to get into her car.

Tom got in, huffed, and leaned his seat back.

“I won’t say a word or make you talk about anything you don’t want to,” Paige said as she pulled out onto the road. “But I want you to know I’ll listen if you need to talk.”

He stayed silent, which gave Paige time to consider Caleb. His hands on her face in the truck after getting back to the Martin’s and as he applied the aloe to her back gave her shivers down her spine. She needed to talk to him about it. She wanted to know where they stood. Progress finally had been made, but their status was unclear. The safe conclusion was he wanted to be friends, just as she suggested. She wanted more from him but if all she got was spending time enjoying his company and being at peace, then she’d take it.

“You know, I didn’t say I expected her to live with me first before we got married,” Tom said, pulling Paige out of her thoughts. “I said there was something to be said for living together first. We’d learn so much about us together if we did.”

“Sorry, Tom, but living together guarantees about as much as getting married civilly or in the temple,” Paige replied.

“What if we decide we’d made a colossal mistake? Why go through this heartache and hassle now just to have it end later?”

Paige had no answer to that one. But the thought came to her, *then why ask Alisa at all if you’re so sure it’s not going to last? Same difference, right?*

"Did you pray or go to the temple before you asked Alisa to marry you?"

"Yes."

"And?"

"And what?"

"Did you get a good feeling about her? Do you think the Lord approved of your choice?"

He rubbed the back of his neck and looked thoughtful for a moment. "Yes, I was confident I'd gotten the answer I needed."

"Then I hope you see what's going on here," Paige said. "We allow our worst doubts and fears to get the better of us because change is scary. But what it boils down to is trust that the Lord has your best interest at heart. It's one thing to say 'Alisa's the one' because you want that so badly to be true. But it's something else to say 'Alisa's it' because the Lord is confirming it's true. It takes faith to follow what you recognize in your heart to be true, despite what outside influences may try to say is false."

"Everything is so crazy, and the more I think about it, the more I'm convinced I'm fooling myself. I can't help feeling like I made a mistake by trying to tie up Alisa's life in my mess. My parents got married in the temple, and they cannot stand each other. They didn't start out that way, but they can barely tolerate being in the same room with each other now. I don't want that with Alisa. Why bother with a temple marriage if there's the possibility we divorce anyway?"

"Are you seriously that convinced you will get divorced?"

"Yes. No. I don't know. I look around me, not just at my parents' marriage, but more Marines than not are working on second and third marriages. Being a Marine wife is rough. How do I know I won't suddenly get a Dear John letter with a packet of divorce papers while I'm deployed in the Middle East? I've seen it happen. More than once."

"You're missing my point," Paige replied. "You're so convinced you will get divorced; did it ever occur to you you're setting yourself up for a self-fulfilling prophecy? And it's not just that. Do you think Heavenly Father made a mistake when he approved of you marrying Alisa?"

His brows furrowed at the suggestion. "No. Of course not, but . . ."

"Alisa loves you. I've never seen her so in love with someone before," Paige said. "I'm not saying that to make you feel guilty. I'm pointing it out so you can understand why a temple marriage is so important to her, beyond being a relatively recent convert. She's chosen you, and she doesn't want anyone else. She doesn't make these kinds of decisions lightly. For you to be saying you might divorce anyway, as if marriage were tissue paper, is probably killing her.

"I'm not saying all this stuff because I love Alisa and I want her to get married at the expense of all else. If it's not right, then it's not right. But Tom, you're a good guy who brought two people into the gospel because of your testimony. But now you're confusing them with these whack ideas. Ideas they'd only experienced in their old life with their parents and extended family. They would have never joined the Church if they wanted to stay that way. But they were both looking for something else, something different. And that's when they found you. I've only known you a short time, but I felt there was a purpose behind it."

"I hear what you're saying, Paige," Tom said, looking out the passenger window.

"Think about it, Tom. You remember what it was like as a missionary. There was no one else but your companion and tons and tons of prayer. This isn't any different, and I don't think the Lord expects you to do anything different. He doesn't give us a spirit of fear, so if you're worried, then you need to consider where that's coming from. I realize I'm sounding like a fireside or conference talk, but maybe you should spend this week really praying about everything. Hard. Or do a session at the temple. I'd be happy to go with you, or Caleb would be happy to go, as well."

"What am I going to do? She'll never forgive me after this," Tom said.

Paige shook her head. "One of the outstanding things about Alisa is she can never stay mad at anyone she loves for very long," Paige replied. "Do me a favor?"

"What's that?"

"Don't fix this today. We're all tired, and well, I'm sunburned, but we've all been out in the sun all day. Tired and slightly dehydrated can equal flared tempers, and both of you need some time to cool off. It might be a good idea if you stayed at my parents' house for the rest of the week. I love the Watsons, but they haven't been making it easy on you. I don't know why it didn't even occur to me to ask sooner."

"I'll consider it," he responded.

Paige looked at the time on her phone. "You have about 40 minutes to decide."

Tom leaned his seat all the way back and closed his eyes. Paige sent up a quick prayer he'd be able to find his way through his maze of doubt and fear. She wished it hadn't hurt Alisa as much as it had. She could only guess what was going through Alisa's mind, especially since her beloved returned-missionary-baptizer was spouting off ideas that could only hurt and confuse her.

He's a big boy, Paige, she thought. *You've said your piece, now let it lie in the Lord's hands. If this works out, it's because it was meant to work out. Hopefully, Tom will do some serious praying. He needs it.*

CHAPTER 25

With all the developments of the day and the long drive back to Bountiful, Paige sighed a huge breath of relief when she finally pulled up to her parents' house. It had been the longest Fourth of July of her life, and it wasn't even over yet.

Paige shook Tom a little.

"Hey, we're here," she said, as he started awake.

"Oh, great," he mumbled. "Your parents wouldn't mind me staying, would they?"

"I'm about ninety-nine percent sure they'd be happy to put you up, but I'd still like to give them the choice," Paige said. "Give me a second to let them know what's up, and I'll be right out. In the meantime, why don't you ask Caleb to grab your stuff, and I'll text Alisa not to freak out."

Tom nodded. He looked tired, even though he'd taken a nap the rest of the drive back. Paige jogged up to the entrance of her parents' home and rushed through the door. "Mom?"

"In the kitchen."

"I have a huge favor to ask," Paige said, then told her mom all the events of the last forty-eight hours.

"Of course, he can stay here," Liz said. "Poor Tom. I understand being upset with your children's choices, but to be so outright hostile to the man who's about to become your son-in-law? There's no excuse for it."

"I wish they felt the same," Paige said as she sent a text to Alisa. "Where do you want him to stay? I can give up my room, and I'll go back to my apartment."

"No, Lindsay's room still has a bed in it, though we were getting ready to paint. I'll get some bed linens and things. Invite him in, and we'll make some dinner. Maybe your dad can talk to him."

"*If* he wants to talk . . . I'm pretty sure he's talked out. Can Dad offer to give him a blessing?"

"That sounds like a splendid idea. Have Caleb come over to help since he's his friend. It'll be good to see Caleb again."

Paige went outside to find Tom leaning on the car.

"My mom is happy to offer you a place to sleep for the week," Paige said. "Come on. I'll show you around."

She led Tom through the front door. "You already know where the front room and kitchen are." She led him down the hallway. "This is where you'll be staying," she said, pointing to the bare room. "My mom is getting some sheets for you. Across the hallway you see the bathroom, and she'll put some towels in there for you to use."

Liz came out of her room with her arms full of bed linens.

"Here let me take those," Tom said, reaching for the sheets. "One thing you learn to do well in boot camp is make your bed."

"Suit yourself," she said. "We're so glad to see you again. When you're ready, Paige and I will get dinner started. I'm sure you're both starving."

"I wanted to thank you both," Tom said. "It's good to find kindness somewhere, even if it's only for a short time."

"No thanks needed, Tom," Liz said. "The Lord is mindful of our needs and blesses us when we need it most. And we're blessed to help, even if it's only in a small way."

He nodded and headed into his room. Paige followed her mother into the kitchen.

"I'll have your father try to talk to him," Liz replied. "He looks downright exhausted and not just physically."

"I agree," Paige said. "He needs something to help build him up again."

Wally walked through the door. "Hun, I found these amazing steaks for a fantastic price. I think I'll fire up the grill tonight."

"That's a fantastic idea," Liz said. "We have an additional guest tonight, so make enough for one more."

"What guest?" He put the steaks in the fridge.

"Follow me, please." It was Liz code for "Come into our room so I can speak with you privately about whatever's going on or whoever is in trouble."

Paige pulled her phone out again. Alisa had sent a long text. But before she read it, Paige texted Caleb.

Would you mind coming over after dinner?
My mom is suggesting my dad give Tom a blessing. We'd like you here to help.

She was in the middle of reading Alisa's text when she got a response from Caleb.

I'll be over around 8

First, she was delighted he was willing. She'd seen converts struggle with exercising the priesthood, like giving blessings. Caleb didn't seem to have that problem. And second, she was excited to see him, period. Butterflies were flitting around in her stomach. Her parents may not tease her out loud, but she wasn't sure she wanted whatever was happening between Caleb and her to be open to questions or speculation. *Act cool, happy, but not too happy to see him. And be normal*, she thought.

Her mom walked into the kitchen. "One thing down. Your dad's in with Tom right now. Now, how did today go? Did you have fun?"

"Caleb and I finally buried the hatchet. As far as what that means, I don't know, but we're not angry with each other anymore and that, more than anything else, feels fantastic."

"Occasionally, I wonder *what if* with you two," Liz mused. "I'm sure he probably resents us. It wasn't easy telling our daughter, who was so obviously in love, she needed to reconsider her choice. It broke my heart to watch you grieve, but I was oh so proud you stuck to your priorities. Seems things have worked out nicely since then."

"Mom, I'll be honest. My heart was always torn about that. Getting married in the temple is super important, but sometimes I wonder if I should have just married Caleb and it might have worked out anyway."

"It's true," Liz said. "It might have. Your road would have been a lot rougher. You both were so young and not on the same page about important things like religion. You've grown in ways separately that you may not have had you stayed together. He joined the Church on his own without pressure from anyone, and you have a career you enjoy and live independently."

Wally and Tom walked into the living room. "Ladies, shall we get some dinner going so we can eat?" Wally asked, pulling the patio door open. "Tom, want to grab those steaks out of the fridge? There's corn on the cob in there too. Meet me out in the backyard."

The next little while was a flurry of food prep. During dinner, Tom talked about life in the Marines and his mission. Tom looked more relaxed and his joking side came out again. Here at the Ellises', he could talk about things and be understood and the topics welcome. The more Tom talked, the more she liked him, and the more she hoped he and Alisa could work it out. He would be great for her. Despite his several missteps, he had a solid testimony of the gospel and would be a strong priesthood holder in his home with Alisa.

Someone knocked on the door just after dinner ended. Paige jumped up to answer it. Caleb stood there with Tom's things.

"You're a little early," she said, taking a bag from him.

"I figured you guys wouldn't mind," Caleb said with a grin.

"Paige, who is it?" Liz called from the other room.

"It's Caleb, Mom," Paige replied.

"Thanks for doing that," Tom said, coming up to the door and giving Caleb a bro hug.

"It's no problem at all," Caleb said.

"How's Alisa?"

"She's asleep," Caleb said. "She didn't want to talk as much as I hoped. I'm sure she didn't want my mom and dad getting hints anything was wrong. As soon as she got home, she told everyone she was exhausted and went right to bed."

Tom nodded.

"Let's move into the living room," Paige suggested. "I'm sure my parents would love to say hi to Caleb."

Wally and Liz stood up as soon as the three entered the room.

"Paige wasn't kidding when she mentioned you'd gotten taller," Wally said as he extended a hand to Caleb. The two men shook hands cordially.

"I think he might have grown an inch or two," Paige smiled.

"Congratulations on Alisa's and your baptism, son," Wally said. "I'm just sorry we never got to tell you in person."

"Thank you," Caleb said. "It's been a lifesaver in more ways than one."

"I never had a chance to give you a hug the last time you were here," Liz said, tears swimming in her eyes. She reached over and pulled him into a tight hug. "I didn't get to talk to you much at Alisa's shower. I'm so overwhelmed. I never thought I'd see the day you'd be a member of the Church."

"Neither did I," Paige said.

"So, Caleb, tell us how you and Tom met and how this all came about," she said, wiping her eyes.

Paige sat down on the room's loveseat, and Caleb took the seat next to her. He put his arm on the back of the couch above her shoulders. She found herself leaning into him. So much for not being obvious, but being this close to him, feeling his warmth around her, she didn't care.

Hearing Caleb and Tom's version of Alisa and Caleb's conversion made her thankful once again they'd met Tom. Because of him, they both had embraced it with a solid foundation.

"Well, gentlemen, let's take care of this blessing," Wally said. "Tom would like it to be private, so we'll go into Tom's room."

Paige sighed when the men left. "I sure hope this helps. He devastated Alisa. I don't think Tom was trying to be intentionally offensive, but I think his fears got the better of him."

"It happens to the best of us," Liz said, getting up and taking a pie out of the oven. "The best way to a man's hurt heart and spirit is through his stomach. Some apple pie à la mode should do the trick."

"I don't know about the men, but that sure makes my heart happy." Paige giggled.

Liz eyed Paige as she scooped ice cream for the slices. "So, there's a part of today's story that's missing, my lovely daughter."

Paige blushed. "Maybe, but everything's so confusing I'm uncertain what to think."

"Honey, if his intentions are what I expect they are, then he'll make them clear soon. Men are straightforward creatures, particularly military men."

"All I know is we're friends. If there's anything more to it, we haven't had time to talk about that," Paige said.

"But he's forgiven you?" Liz asked.

"Yes. He told me since joining the Church he understands what I had been trying to say. He could have saved me years of guilt if he had told me that sooner, but I don't fault him for holding on to some hurt. Now I'm not positive where we stand, but at least there's no longer any anger and guilt. That by itself makes him coming back to Utah worth it."

"Well, I'm glad things are finally looking a lot better between the two of you," Liz said, a small smile on her face.

"Yes, well, we're a week away from him going back in South Carolina," Paige said. "We may get along now, but that doesn't change the fact our lives are very separate."

"True, but what is distance when you know it's right? What would you do if he proposed to you tomorrow? And don't give me that look, my darling daughter, I may be a lot of things, but unobservant isn't one of them."

Paige sighed. "I might seriously consider saying yes. We're not still the same as we were, but I'm glad we're not—because we've grown up so much since then. And I respect him a lot more now. He worked hard to get his officer's commission. He enjoys what he does, and he's strong in the gospel. That's an impressive resume. But again—me, here; him, South Carolina."

"That's the part you might be overthinking, my love. He's grown to be an excellent young man. A young man who, if my suspicions are right, knows exactly what he wants. Now he has to put himself in a position to get it."

Paige shook her head. "You're just like him. Incorrigible."

The men filed back into the kitchen. Liz started handing out the bowls of pie. Paige looked at Caleb. He didn't stop looking at her, and there was a strange, soft look in his eyes when their eyes met. It gave Paige goosebumps.

Sooner than she would have wished, Caleb was saying goodnight. "It was a genuine pleasure to catch up with you both. And thank you for the pie, Liz. It was amazing."

"You're always welcome here, Caleb," Liz replied. "I hope you know that."

"Thank you."

"I'm going to walk Caleb out," Paige said.

They stood on the front porch.

"You may not see me very much this week. I feel like I need to be with Lise right now," Caleb said. "Tom and I will probably do a bro session over at the Bountiful temple. I didn't want you to think I was avoiding you."

"I understand," she replied. "If you or Lise need anything, I'm available. I want everything to work out for her and Tom."

"Just keep praying for them," he said. "I think we're all going to need it."

Paige nodded and smiled. She looked up into his handsome face. She observed every bit to remember when he left. Time was so short, and he'd be gone so soon. He may not be feeling the same way she was, but she was glad he was with her here now. So much time had passed, and yet in this moment she still felt like that eighteen-year-old girl standing on this same porch, looking into those hazel eyes, saying goodnight. Except back then, the goodbye usually came with a head-whirling kiss. Tonight, she'd have to settle for basking in his brilliant smile that was for her only.

"You're pretty amazing, Paige," Caleb said. "I'm glad we got to know each other again. Through all this, seems like you've been the only voice of reason."

"You forget," she said. "I'm a smarty-pants. I only talk a good game most of the time."

"Well, whatever it is, I was glad you were there," he said. "Goodnight, Paige."

"Good night, Caleb." She wrapped her arms around him and laid her head against his chest. They stood there for a while, enjoying being close to each other. She wished Caleb would kiss her, but they'd only just gone back to being friends. She didn't want to make things awkward by rushing him. Instead, when she let go, she shoved his shoulder to get him off the porch and send him home.

Chapter 26

Alisa and Paige were discussing the final plan for the morning of the wedding in the Watson's kitchen, except Alisa didn't really take part. It was Paige making all the plans and Alisa nodding her head. Paige leaned against the refrigerator.

"Lise," Paige said, grabbing her friend's hand. "Haven't you and Tom talked yet?"

"Not really," Alisa said. "And it's because I don't know what to say. Paige, I've been on my knees every night, praying something will come to me, because I'm not sure how to feel. I love Tom and I want to marry him. He's got so many good things about him, but this living together thing, it seems so unlike him. The *him* I thought I knew. Are there other things he might have hidden from me? If he did, he's not likely to confess them."

"When I talked to him, he said he was just thinking aloud. Not that that excuses him, but I don't think he was serious. His parents did such a bang-up job of screwing him up about marriage. I mean, it's easy to see why he'd be a little gun shy. His timing couldn't have been worse."

"You're telling me. We're getting married in a couple of days, and I'm so confused. I don't want to end up making a huge mistake that I'll regret later just for the sake of the wedding."

A knock came at the door. Paige heard Alisa say, "Oh, hi. Come in, please."

Paige peeked around the corner and saw Tom with two people she didn't know. Paige peeked her head back in the kitchen. Of all the awkward situations to find herself in! She didn't want to make a big show by leaving, but she probably shouldn't be there at all.

"Mom, Dad, this is my fiancé, Alisa Watson. Alisa, this is my mom, Constance Avery."

"She's just lovely, Tom," Constance said. "Thank you for having us over."

"Uh, you're welcome," Alisa said.

"And this is my dad, Craig Fields."

"Please make yourselves comfortable," Alisa said.

"Tom," Craig said. "Your mother and I have been doing a lot of talking over the last twenty-four hours. We've decided that for a few days, we'll put aside our differences for the sake of your wedding."

"Uh, I'm speechless," Tom said. "Thank you, I guess."

"Yes, thank you," Alisa said. "Tom's been under a lot of stress these last few weeks. It's not all your fault. Neither of you were here for most of it. But some of the stress was your fault. I don't wish to seem ungrateful or unappreciative of your gesture, but I hope you understand your son's side of things. He's been in the middle of the both of you his whole life. He loves you both and sometimes it seems like you're asking him to pick sides and that's not fair. I'll probably get in trouble with Tom for saying so later, but I have to. I love him, and I hope you love him enough to keep your word."

Paige felt like cheering. Alisa usually didn't back down from a challenge, especially for someone she loved. Paige was so proud to be present as Alisa stood up for Tom. She peeked around the corner again. Constance sat in a chair nearby and looked to Craig. Craig stood there, arms folded. Constance was definitely Tom's mother. The familial resemblance was strong. She had tight curly hair she wore short with russet-brown skin that was several shades darker than Tom's. For Craig's part, it seemed the only thing Tom inherited from him was his intense eyes and tall stature.

Alisa's voice cracked. "I don't see how two people could go from loving one another and looking forward to marrying in the temple and then act so hateful to each other later." Alisa sniffed.

"That's not simple to explain," Constance said. "Especially when it involves answers that will probably only cause a fight. And I don't want to do that. So, I'll say what I think, and then maybe Craig can either agree with me or tell you his side."

Craig nodded.

"One thing I can tell you is that we started out with love," she said. "We wanted what everyone else wanted—that forever family. But sometimes when you're young you don't always see things about the person you love beforehand enough to make you prudent. You don't get married because you expect to be arguing all the time or that you'll end up divorced. I only speak for myself when I say I chose to get married. Craig attracted me, and we seemed to have some things in common on the surface. It wasn't until after we got married that we discovered our . . . differences. Then the differences became problems, and then we're fighting all the time. We thought maybe having you, Tom, would fix things, but in the end, it was evident our marriage wouldn't make it. Craig?"

"That about sums it up."

Constance nodded. "It's probably too late to say this, but don't let our marriage be your guide. If you both truly love each other, then just work toward loving each other as much as you can every day. Your father and I believed we were in love, but there are some differences love can't make up for. We rushed into everything. Maybe if we had slowed down a bit, given ourselves time to get to know each other better, then things might have been different.

"And, Alisa, we both do love Tom. We don't regret having him. He'll be our son forever because we made that covenant before he was born. If anything good came out of the disaster of our marriage, it was you, son. We've put you in the middle often, but we both love you very much. We're proud of the man you've become, and now we're even prouder you've found such a beautiful girl to share your life with. As for myself, I'm excited I'll get some gorgeous grandbabies."

Tom had remained silent during the conversation, but once his mother had finished Paige could hear an enormous sigh. He walked toward the front door. "I need a minute." Out he walked and slammed the door behind him.

Alisa only hesitated for a moment before she stood up. "I need to—" She rushed out the door after Tom.

The silence in the room was deafening. She walked out from the kitchen and waved a shy hand at Tom's parents.

"I'm sorry," Paige said, her cheeks reddened. "I really didn't mean to eavesdrop, but I was in the kitchen when you showed up. I guess Alisa thought she didn't have time to introduce me. I'm Paige. I'm Alisa's best friend and the maid of honor."

They mumbled their greetings, but it was clear they too were uncomfortable.

"So, I hope I'm not out of turn while Alisa and Tom take a minute, but I wanted to thank you both for Tom. Alisa's been my best friend since high school and never in all the years I've known her have I seen her more in love with anyone. And I've been witness to the caring and compassionate person Tom is.

"His example and testimony brought not only Alisa, but her brother, Caleb, into the Church. That's something not a single person who has known the Watsons would have believed possible."

"Thank you," Constance said. "I'm grateful to hear that."

Paige heard Craig sniff a little, but she didn't dare look at him. She didn't want to embarrass him at the moment.

"No matter what, he is a great guy. Everyone I've talked to, including Caleb, says he's a good Marine and a skilled pilot. That's something to be proud of. I've only known him a few weeks, and I know I am."

The front door opened back up and Alisa walked through. She started when she saw Paige.

"I sort of introduced myself," Paige said sheepishly. "Do you want me to go?"

Alisa shook her head and sat down on the couch she'd just vacated. She looked at her future in-laws.

"So, let's talk logistics," Alisa said, glancing toward the front door. "Are either of you going to be in the temple with us?"

"I will be," Constance said. She looked over at Craig.

"I won't," he said. "I'll be waiting outside for you both."

"Okay," Alisa said. "You could probably stand near my parents since they won't be coming in either. Might be nice for them to have another family member with them."

He nodded.

Paige listened as Alisa talked with these two people. Were she in Tom's shoes, Paige might very well consider marriage the way he had. Getting married was a big step whether you were LDS or not. And Constance had been right when she said it was better to see you'd made the right choice beforehand. Paige reflected on the question her mother asked a couple of days ago—if Caleb were to ask her tomorrow to marry him, what would Paige say? Paige felt she'd have no hesitation about saying yes to him. Not because he was one of the most handsome men she'd ever known. Not because he got to wear a fancy blue uniform on special occasions. But because she appreciated the person Caleb was. He was good. He was responsible. He had a deep testimony of the gospel. And he could make her laugh like no one else had been able to.

The front door opened, and Tom walked back in. He sat down next to Alisa. "Your mom is going to be in the sealing room with us, and your dad will be with my mom and dad outside."

Tom nodded and held Alisa's hand. "Sounds good. Alisa and I are taking you both out to dinner tonight. We figured a steakhouse is pretty neutral. Any objections?"

Both his parents shook their heads.

"Have you met Paige?" Tom asked.

"They have," Paige said.

“Fine, then I will leave Alisa to do whatever it is she was doing before we came over. I’m going back over to Paige’s house to get ready for dinner. Either one of you is welcome to join me, and meet Paige’s parents.”

“I think we ought to let your mom know about the plan for the day so she can know where she needs to be,” Alisa said, giving Tom a tentative smile. “Text me when it’s time to go?”

Tom nodded. “Come on, Dad. I’m sure Wally would love to meet you.”

Paige watched the men go and the tension in the air decreased by a lot. Paige wondered how Tom had grown up with that all the time. But he was moving on to a new life with Alisa where hopefully with a lot of prayer and a temple visit the next day, he could work through some of his problems.

CHAPTER 27

Caleb sat on the front porch of the Ellises' with Paige the next day. It was a companionable silence between them as they waited for Tom to finish getting ready. Caleb and Tom were going to do a session at the temple, something Paige knew Tom needed badly. Hope warred with agitation as she sat next to Caleb. A few times she'd almost looked at him and said, "Okay, what's your deal?" but then she'd stop herself. Now wasn't the time. He'd said they were friends, but nothing more. There had been no declarations of undying love for her, so she would have to exercise a bit more patience. Patience was torture at this point.

"He'll be okay, right?" Paige asked Caleb.

"Yeah. Once we get done this morning, he'll probably do better," Caleb said.

"Do you want to text me when you're done? Maybe we can have them meet if that's what Tom wants," Paige said. "I hate watching Alisa be so miserable."

"I'll text you," he said. "It's so weird how things seem to have worked out. I wouldn't have guessed in a million years that we'd be wondering if there would still be a wedding. Not with the way Tom feels for Alisa. But then again, I also didn't think things would change between us. I'm not certain if that's because I didn't want them to or if it was easier to keep my distance by being mad. But turns out, I'm really relieved and happy we're not at odds anymore."

She grabbed his hand. "Me too. It's nice to have that burden lifted and discover that even if we're more grown up, there are some things that haven't changed."

"Like what?" he grinned.

"Um, like threatening to throw me in the sprinklers," she said.

"You nearly deserved that."

"I beg your pardon. I wasn't the one running around kissing nineteen-year-olds."

Caleb laughed. "Honestly, she totally caught me off guard. Your face. I worried for a moment you might actually run us over with your car."

"Be glad I didn't think of it at the time. I would have been sorely tempted," Paige said. "No matter what I thought about it, I knew it was none of my business. You're a grown man. You didn't have to ask permission to do anything, least of all from me."

"The honest truth is, if I had known she would try it, I probably wouldn't have let her. There was this other girl I had my eye on. I wasn't sure if we'd get along well enough to make anything work, so I figured I had nothing to lose."

"You don't have to explain yourself," she said. "Besides, I'm the superior kisser anyway."

"Really? That confident?"

"I seem to recall someone wasn't complaining the night of prom. And I have ten more years' experience."

"With who?"

"A lady never reveals her secrets."

"Now I know you're teasing—"

Tom opened the front door and came out on the porch with them. He was dressed in Sunday best.

"I'm ready to go." He looked rested and calm.

"Okay, let's get going then," Caleb said. He glanced over at Paige.

Paige smiled. "Have a good session."

Paige walked back in the house and headed to her room when her phone rang. It was Elliot. She took in a heavy breath. This was about to get really awkward.

"Hi, Paige," Elliot's cheery voice came on the other end of the line. Paige cringed.

"Hi," Paige answered. "Could you meet me over at the reflection pool? That's probably the easiest for you."

Paige looked up at the temple. Alisa should be there the day after tomorrow. Paige could only hope it would work out as planned. But that was between Tom and the Lord.

"Hi," Elliot said, coming up to stand next to her.

"Hi, there," Paige said. "This is where Alisa is getting married. She called it a fairy-tale castle."

"She's not wrong. It looks like one," Elliot said. He wandered over to the seating by the pool. "I have a feeling I won't like what you're going to tell me."

Paige gave him a sad smile and moved to sit next to him. "I think you're right. But I wanted to give you the courtesy of telling you to your face since you've always been very kind and patient with my lateness."

"The Marine?" he asked.

Paige nodded. "It's amazing how time and distance can pull people apart, but there are some things that never really change."

"Well, I can't say I'm not disappointed," he said. "I had a feeling when I met him, I'd probably lost out on my chance. I stuck around to see if I was wrong."

"You're a really great guy, and someday you'll find a girl lucky enough to go there with you."

"I will, someday," Elliot said, giving Paige a slight smile. "I have faith everything will work out the way it's supposed to. Just like they did for you."

"Thanks," Paige said.

Elliot stood up and pulled Paige up with him. He hugged her. "Good luck wherever this path takes you."

"And I'll make sure I smack Caleb for you for doing the whole macho *who's got the tighter grip* handshake thing."

Elliot laughed. "Do that. Though I think I might have surprised him if I had been ready for it."

Paige lay across the couch of her parents' living room. She'd been texting Alisa trying to distract her from the whole thing with Tom. Even though she'd told her about Tom's blessing and his current trip to the temple with Caleb, Alisa's responses lacked any enthusiasm. Paige was heartbroken for her friend. It reminded her of the night before prom their senior year. Paige was in Alisa's room talking about her prom dress until she was taken by surprise when Alisa broke down into tears.

"I'm so happy for you guys, I really am," Alisa had said. "But sometimes, knowing you guys have an automatic date to stuff just sucks. I can't go with you because no one's asked me, and Brent's taking someone else. Not that I expected Brent to, but at least that would have been fun to go on a friend date. So, I get to sit at home and wait for you guys to get back."

Paige had hugged Alisa then, not knowing what to say. She learned that night that as much as Paige and Caleb considered her part of their group, she felt outside it. And this thing with Tom was really feeling like that. Here Paige was enjoying being around Caleb again, and Alisa was once again trying to figure out where she fit into all of it. The worst of it was this was supposed to be Alisa's time—the happiest time of her life.

A knock came at the door. Paige swung her feet off the couch and paused only a second to send a heart emoji to Alisa before she answered the door. Tom and Caleb stood there.

"Hi, guys," Paige said. "Back from the temple already?"

"Yes," Tom said as he walked through the door. There was an energy to him that hadn't been there before. "I need your help, but let me drop my stuff off really quick." He disappeared into his room and shut the door.

Paige looked at Caleb. "What was that all about?"

"Your guess is as good as mine," Caleb said. "It's the first thing he's said since we left the temple. He was really quiet on the way back."

"Come out of the foyer, then," she said, motioning him to the couch. She sat down, tucking a foot under her as Caleb sat down next to her. "I've been texting Alisa. She's really down right now. I've been trying to encourage her, but I know it's been hard for her. I wish there was something I could do to help comfort her."

"That's actually what I was going to ask your help for," Tom said, coming back into the living room. "I've messed up pretty badly. I've said some things I didn't really mean. And yes, I've been stressed out, but that doesn't excuse me for taking it out on her. She's the one I want to be with for the rest of my life and beyond, and what do I do? I did stuff I watched my parents do to each other. Stuff I swore I'd never do to the woman I married."

He pulled his hands through his hair.

"I need to do something. Something that expresses to her how sorry I am. Tells her I honestly didn't mean a word I said. That I couldn't imagine living my life without her. I mean, if that means I had to hire a sixteen-piece Mariachi band and serenade her at midnight I would."

"You don't need to go that far," Paige said, giggling. "But Lise enjoys being shown how much you love her as much as you telling her."

Her brain started working. She reflected on her earlier memory of prom and Alisa's disappointment at not being able to go.

"Just one second," Paige said. "I might have an idea."

Paige did a quick search on her phone and then after a minute looked up with an enormous smile on her face. She stood up and walked over to the kitchen table. She grabbed a pad of paper and a pencil and wrote some notes down. She motioned the men to come over.

"*Operation: Dog House* has begun," she said. "Here's the plan, gentlemen. You go gather these items, and I'll explain the next part of the plan when you get back."

CHAPTER 28

When Tom and Caleb returned, they laid out the items Paige had requested. There were blue and red balloons, a blank greeting card, pages of printed pictures of Alisa and Tom, and a teddy bear.

Paige snatched the bear off the table and hugged it to her. "I love it!" The bear wore Marine dress blues. "Where did you find this?"

"A knickknack shop next to the copy center we went to," Caleb said. "You asked for a teddy bear, and this is a teddy bear."

She gave him a big smile.

"Okay, next part. Caleb will cut out all the pictures. Tom, you write on the back of each one something about Lise you love or a reason you wanted to marry her. On the greeting card, I want you to write something sweet to her."

She placed a pile of colored markers in front of them. "Can't be an elementary school teacher without a stash of coloring implements."

"Okay, I'm still not seeing where this is going." Tom said.

"You will," Paige said grinning.

"No hint?" Tom asked.

"You know, the longer you take to think of things to write to Lise, the longer she'll have to wait. Do you need help?"

"No," Tom said, narrowing his eyes at her. "I can think of reasons I want to marry her. Lots of them."

She waved her hands at him. "Then please continue."

Tom sighed and started writing on the back of the pictures.

Paige grabbed the envelope of the greeting card and started drawing on it. Caleb leaned over to her as he cut out another picture.

"You came up with this an hour ago?" Caleb said.

"Yes," Paige said. "Did you know Alisa didn't go to prom?"

He thought about it for a minute. "I think . . . I . . . did? Wait. No. No, she didn't. I thought Brent took her for some reason."

"Nope, he went with that girl in our ward," Paige said, drawing hearts and flourishes on the envelope. "You know, I had a ton of fun with you that night. I had a ton of fun with you in high school, period. But in all that time I didn't consider once Lise wasn't having any fun, or that she was feeling left out. She was good at keeping it to herself because she loved the both of us so much. And it seems like she's doing it again because she wants everyone to be happy, but her argument with Tom was too much."

"But that wasn't the cause of our problems," Tom said.

"I know, but having Caleb and me arguing with each other wasn't helping anything either. You know what that's like, Tom. Feeling like you have to choose between two people you love equally who are always fighting with each other. And she probably thought she was dealing with the *Paige and Caleb Show* again instead of this being about her. It's not fair, and I love her too much to let her be on the outside. Not now. She's days away from getting married to the first man I've seen make her smile so big it probably hurts her face. She needs to feel special and loved and the center of the freaking universe to everyone around her because she deserves it. She always does that for everyone else.

"We can do something about it, so that's what we're doing."

Caleb bumped her shoulder and gave her a soft smile. She returned it.

After all the pictures were written on, rolled and stuffed in the balloons, Paige handed Tom the card.

"Okay, phase three of *Operation: Dog House*, Tom. Write something super sweet and romantic on the card, but really that's more of a keepsake than anything. What you say to her when you get to her house will be way more important.

"Then you need to look good. Like, really good. So I'm going to get you an iron, ironing board, and some starch, and then Caleb and I are going to get these balloons filled. You, sir, are going to air out your uniform. While we're gone, press it and then we'll be ready for phase four when we get back.

"Wait, we're giving her a balloon bouquet?"

Paige picked the Marine bear off the table with the attached card. It said, "Life without you would be un-Bear-able."

Caleb started laughing. Tom scrunched his nose up.

"Isn't that kind of cheesy?" Tom asked.

"Yes," Paige said. "And Lise will eat it up with a spoon."

"That is a genius idea, Paige," Caleb said. "Believe me, brother, Lise will love it."

"If you guys say so," Tom said. "I'm willing to try anything. Is Paige always this bossy?"

"You have no idea," Caleb said with a smile. Paige kicked him as he walked by her.

They were almost to Paige's car when Paige smacked Caleb on the shoulder.

"Hey! What is all this abuse?"

"For nearly breaking Elliot's hand when you met him," Paige said, trying to look serious.

"I can't help it if I have such manly hands. I don't know my own strength, I guess. So, you talked to Elliot, did you?"

"Yup. I told him I couldn't see him anymore. He took it surprisingly well."

"Sounds like a classy guy."

"I'd say so. I informed him there was someone else. That I hoped he'd find a special girl to take to the temple someday. That just wasn't me." He held the driver's side door open for her and then got in himself.

"So, no more Elliot. Poor guy," Caleb said, shaking his head. "Have you started dating someone else?"

"Not yet, but I have a prospect that's looking good so far."

"Should I be worried?"

"Yes. He's tall, good looking, an all-around good guy, and has a job he loves. I think you'd like him."

"What's his problem then? Seems to me you should have already gotten together, if he's so great."

"Not sure if he's entirely made up his mind yet."

"I wouldn't be so sure."

She smiled over at him. "How did the temple go?"

"Good. I couldn't speak for him since he didn't talk much before or after. He seemed more relaxed coming out than he did going in. I think he got the answers he was looking for."

"Good. I'm glad. I was there when his parents came over to your house. They looked like they were trying really hard to keep the peace between themselves, so that's one less thing he needs to stress over."

"I'm glad they're trying."

"I hope everything works out for both Alisa's and Tom's sakes," Paige said. "We need to get this one last thing resolved and get them married. Let's hope everyone is on their best behavior until we send them on their honeymoon."

Caleb nodded. "All this family drama's been making things hard, but hopefully this thing we're doing will help them sort that out. His love for her was never in question."

"That's why when I say yes to whoever gets around to asking me to marry him, I'm going to be one hundred percent sure."

Caleb examined her face. "I would hope so."

The trip to the party store and back felt like a mini-date. He opened doors for her, they pushed each other around like kids, and laughed together when they tried shoving the floating balloons that refused to get into her car.

There was any easiness between them, which was a nice change of pace since he'd arrived. She had a strong sense of peace when she was around Caleb that told her everything was working out like it was supposed to. That still didn't stop her from having one small nagging worry in the back of her mind.

Was she expecting too much from Caleb? He'd been nothing but sweet and courteous, but he'd never once mentioned getting back together. He'd said they were friends and maybe that should be enough for her. Except it wouldn't be. Being close to Caleb had brought back a number of the dreams she'd had before about what life together would look like. The dreams were updated now since they were older and in different places in their lives, but some things remained the same. She imagined the way they would be together—him making her laugh until her stomach hurt, and him still that sweet and teasing guy. She saw the children they could have together and the wonderful father he'd be to them. He would honor all the promises and covenants he'd make to her and the Lord to make sure they stayed together for eternity. She longed for that life, and it wouldn't be the same if it wasn't with him. But you couldn't force someone to love you or return feelings they didn't have. So, she had to hope that this sense of peace meant she needed to be a bit more patient.

They parked in her driveway, but neither seemed to be in a big hurry to get out of the car.

"Just a little over twenty-four hours from now everything will be different," Caleb said. "Will you be ready for that?"

"Yes. I've been doing a lot of praying that things will go the way they should. Can't say I'm a huge fan of all this waiting around to see how it plays out. But I know the Lord sees the bigger picture and knows exactly how it should be."

"Some guy will be extremely lucky when he takes you through the temple," he said.

Paige smiled sadly at him. Not exactly the words she wanted to hear from him. She wanted so badly to say, *"Why can't you be that lucky guy?"*

"Should we finish *Operation: Dog House*?"

"After you, Miss Ellis," he said, taking her hand and giving it a squeeze.

The three stood on the sidewalk outside the Watson home. Paige swiped down Tom's uniform and made sure everything was in place.

"She has no idea we're here. You ready?" Paige asked

"What are you guys going to do?" Tom asked, a nervous tenor to his voice.

"We're going to stand right here until it becomes extremely inappropriate," Paige said.

Caleb laughed.

"Here goes," Tom said, taking in a deep breath. He walked toward the house with a perfect Marine bearing.

"You think he'll be okay?" Paige whispered to Caleb.

He put his arm around her waist. "If he doesn't pass out, he'll be fine."

"He would?" Paige asked, horrified.

"Probably not. He's a Marine. But you never know."

She leaned into Caleb's side and watched as Tom knocked on the door and waited.

Ted answered the door.

"Sir, I'd like to take a moment to talk to your daughter, please?" Tom asked.

The expression on Ted's face alone was worth all the trouble they'd gone to. He disappeared and a second later Alisa took his place.

"Tom, what are you . . .?" Even at their distance, her gasp was audible.

Tom knelt down in front of her. "Alisa, I've been such an idiot. I've treated you badly and said things that should have never come out of my mouth, let alone directed at you. I love you. From the first moment I saw you, I knew you would be important in my life. I didn't know why, but I knew I needed to get to know you, see what kind of woman you were. You were everything I could have hoped for. You were strong, loving, caring, talented, and you certainly didn't put up with any crap. I loved that about you. It told me you'd be honest and forthright.

"I'm asking you to forgive me. I promise to work hard every day to be the man that you need. Would you be my wife? Would you consider showing up to our wedding on Friday?"

Alisa surged forward, wrapping herself around Tom.

Caleb turned them around on the sidewalk and they headed back toward the Ellises'.

"Well, I guess that took care of that part," he said, smiling.

Paige giggled. "I'd say so. I'm so glad. I've been so sick for her."

"I agree," he said. She put her arm through his as they walked down the sidewalk.

"These weeks have been some of the weirdest but funnest days I've had in a long time. Most of it because of you, Caleb."

"You mean stressful, irritating, and frustrating?"

"Caleb, you are all those things sometimes, but all the rest of it more than makes up for the other stuff. And I'm glad we had time to reconnect."

"And here I thought you were glad to get rid of me in a few days," he said, smirking.

"I may have said that, but I didn't mean it," she said. "Things will be a lot duller when you go home."

When they got to her house, she reached up and hugged him before going through the door. She turned to take one last glimpse of Caleb and smiled when she saw him giving her that soft expression that gave her goosebumps.

"Good night, Paige," he said. "See you the morning of the wedding."

Chapter 29

Paige woke up at the crack of dawn the morning of the wedding. Hair in huge curlers, make-up, dress, and beauty supply bags in tow, she made her way to the Watsons' house. Karen let her in, looking as frazzled as she'd ever seen her.

"Paige, you need to talk some sense into my daughter," Karen said. "She's been sitting on her bed since who knows when—texting Tom—and it's driving me crazy. We've got so much to do!"

"I'm on it, Mrs. Watson," Paige said. She flew to Alisa's bedroom. She was looking at her phone, laughing. Paige dumped all her stuff on Alisa's bed and narrowed her eyes at the giggling bride.

"Seriously?" Paige tapped her foot.

"What? Tom just said the cutest thing—"

"Focus," Paige said, nudging her friend with her foot. "And you better not be sending selfies to each other because that counts as seeing the bride before the wedding."

"Fine, I'm getting up," Alisa said.

Paige took her by the shoulders and shoved her toward the bathroom. "Shower, body wash, shampoo and conditioner, lotion, perfume, getting-ready clothes, make-up, hair, jewelry, and then dress. Then we have to leave so we can be early."

Paige stepped out of the room for a moment to grab Alisa a towel. She came back to find Alisa staring at her phone and giggling again.

"Mine," Paige said as she plucked the phone out of Alisa's hand.

"But—"

"He'll be fine. He doesn't have as much crap to do to get ready. Putting on a uniform and styling his hair will not take three hours, but your stuff will. Chop, chop."

"You know I love it *and* I hate it when you're bossy," Alisa said.

"I'm trying to keep your mom happy. She's running around like a cat in a bath."

Alisa finally made it into the shower, and Paige hurried to find Karen. "Mrs. Watson, I finally got Alisa going. Is there anything—"

Paige stopped dead in her tracks. Caleb stood there in full dress blues, white hat, and gloves. He looked at her with his smirky grin, looking more handsome than she'd ever seen him. It literally took her breath away. Time stopped for a fraction of a second as her lungs finally caught up with her racing heart. Then she realized the mess of curlers on her head.

She screeched and sprinted for the hallway. "Don't look at me. I'm a mess."

She heard him laughing.

"Don't worry," he said, loudly. "I was just leaving, anyway."

"Paige?" Karen's voice came from the living room. "Did you call me?"

"Yes, before Caleb got an eyeful of my pre-wedding mess. I was wondering if you need help with anything while Alisa's in the shower."

"I'm sure Caleb didn't even think twice about it," Karen said. "I have a question, or a few questions."

"Okay."

"So the wedding time is 1 p.m. We have to be at the temple an hour and a half early. Then the ceremony or whatever it is. And then they come out?"

"Yes. Stand with the photographer. Even if they may not be LDS, they've probably done a million LDS weddings and know the drill."

Karen's eyes filled with tears. "I wish I could be there for her."

"You will be. She'll be looking for you and Mr. Watson first thing."

"Small comfort."

Paige gave Karen a brief hug. "It'll be a marvelous day. And then we'll do the ring ceremony as soon as we get to the reception hall, so Mr. Watson can walk Alisa down the aisle. They even wrote some vows to read before they exchanged the rings."

Karen nodded, but didn't look very comforted.

Paige and Karen were in the middle of getting Alisa's makeup and hair done when there was a knock at the door.

"Someone's knocking at this time in the morning?" Karen said. "Alisa, are you expecting anyone?"

"No, everyone's here that should be here."

Ted walked into the room carrying two very large vases of roses.

"Aww, did Tom send those to you?" Paige said, smelling the flowers once Ted put them down.

She pulled the card attached to the red roses. It was addressed to Alisa. She handed her the note. "He sure did. That's awesome. What a sweet thing to do."

Paige turned to the other set of roses. "I bet these are for you, Karen."

The roses were beautiful—yellow with red edges. Paige pulled the card off the other bouquet. She had to do a double take. It said her name. Blood rushed to her cheeks.

"Is the other bouquet for me too?" Alisa asked.

"No, they're for me."

Alisa's Cheshire smile spread from ear to ear. Where Alisa's card was merely a single piece of printed cardstock, Paige's was fatter and heavier.

"I'm going to go read this in the hallway," Paige said, barely registering the shooing waves she was getting from Alisa. She stood in the doorway of Caleb's room. With shaking fingers, she opened the envelope.

"Paige, I hardly know where to start. It's been a wild ride these last few weeks, but I wouldn't change them for anything. I heard you talking to your mom the other day. Sorry, not sorry, I was eavesdropping after we gave Tom the blessing. I figured at best we could be good friends after all this. After hearing you talk to your mom, I have hope now that maybe we could be more. I never forgot you, Paige. Not because you were Lise's best friend. But because I could never find anyone sassy enough, smarty-pants enough, kind enough, or courageous as you. It just wasn't fair to any of the other women I dated because I constantly compared them to you. Please tell me you feel the same way. Give me hope I can take you through the temple to be mine for eternity. This man is no longer that boy you used to know. He's finally got his head on straight, and now he sees exactly what he wants in you, if Heavenly Father will bless him with it. I love you, Paige Ellis. I always have, and I always will. Love, Caleb.

Paige wiped away her tears and read the note two more times. She hardly believed what she was reading. She pulled out her phone to text Caleb when she noticed the alarm for leaving the house for the temple had been going off.

"Lise, we have to hurry!" She turned around to see Alisa in her wedding dress. Paige couldn't hold back the tears once Karen attached the veil. "Oh, Lise, you are so beautiful."

"Stop crying! You'll make me cry, and then I'll ruin this beautiful makeup job Mom did."

Paige grabbed her best friend and hugged her tightly.

"Are you all right?" Alisa asked, hugging back. "Who were the flowers from?"

"He loves me, Lise," Paige said. "He said he loves me. My heart is so full. Seriously, this is the happiest I've ever been. I wish I had time to tell him."

"Of course, he loves you," Alisa said. "I saw that the minute he saw you at the airport. He may have been able to fool everyone else, including himself, but he couldn't fool me."

"We have to get going!" Paige squeaked. "Karen, can you or Ted drive? I can do my hair and makeup in the car."

After Paige slipped on her bridesmaid dress, everyone bundled into the Watson's car and zoomed toward Salt Lake City. Paige fanned her face every so often to keep from crying. Caleb loved her. He always had, and he always would. Her heart jumped around behind her ribcage. The enormous smile refused to leave her face, and she felt impatient to see Caleb.

CHAPTER 30

The craziness only intensified as they got to the temple. There was parking to find, helping the Watsons find the temple grounds, finding the right entrance door, and getting temple recommends out. Alisa hugged and kissed her parents and then sprinted for the entrance to the temple. Spending a few precious minutes in the temple's bride's room allowed them to slow down and take a breath.

"What did Caleb say?" Alisa asked as Paige helped her with the sleeve inserts for her dress.

"He said he's always loved me and he's going to ask me to marry him," Paige said, grabbing a tissue from a box nearby. "I couldn't be happier, Lise. We talked on the way down from Logan. Like, really talked. He forgave me for the past, and he asked me to forgive him for being too prideful to tell me he understood. I hoped he would want to see if there was something there between us still, but he hadn't said a word about it until today. If he asks me to marry him, then we're going to be sisters finally."

"Not that we needed marriage licenses for that."

Paige hugged Alisa when an elderly temple worker approached them.

"Are you girls ready?" she asked.

They straightened out Alisa's dress and checked her sleeves before turning to a mirror to make sure she hadn't gotten makeup everywhere. The cute older lady escorted them into the sealing room.

As soon as Paige locked eyes with Caleb, she couldn't see anything else, and she didn't want to. She memorized every detail of his face—his bright hazel eyes, his smirky half grin, his dark, short cropped hair brushed to the side. All of it was enhanced by the Sunday clothes he wore and the happiness that radiated from him in this holy place. It threatened to stop her heart a few times, but she drank it in.

Finally, the sealer announced Tom and Alisa as husband and wife. Everyone stood up to congratulate the couple while the temple workers shooed them out of the room. But Paige didn't go up to Alisa. She'd do that outside. The only person she wished to be near was Caleb. She crossed the room to him and took his hand in hers. "I got your flowers," she said, leaning into him for his ears only. He looked down at her and smiled.

"Good, I hoped they would get there on time," he said, entwining their fingers together.

They followed Tom and Alisa as they walked outside the temple doors. Alisa ran straight to her mom and dad.

"Oh, honey, you look so radiant," Karen cried.

"I feel radiant, Mom. I'm so happy right now it's not fair to everyone else."

They stiffly shook Tom's hand, before the photographer started corralling everyone around to get pictures.

Paige felt impatient. Pictures were her least favorite part of the wedding. They took forever, and they separated her and Caleb from each other mostly, when all she craved was to be near him. But finally the photographer dragged Tom and Alisa off to do the bride and groom pictures. Paige and Caleb were able to stand next to each other again. She put her hand in his. She glanced over to where Karen and Ted stood. Karen watched them with a grimace on her face, but otherwise didn't approach or talk to them.

Paige and Caleb wandered over to the reflection pool. The normally smooth water rippled a little with the slight breeze that blew, and Paige looked down to see her and Caleb standing together. Tears welled up in her eyes looking at the image. Caleb's gloved hand put a finger under her chin so she looked at him.

"You okay?" he asked softly.

"I've never been happier in my life," she said, smiling up at him. "I've never felt so blessed, or so lucky it's you. All those years apart and no one could compare to you either. Now I'm glad they couldn't. I don't want to go through life with anyone else."

Caleb leaned his head down and softly touched his lips to hers. Explosions of butterflies burst all over her as her heart skipped beats to have him kissing her like this. She wrapped an arm around his neck and his solid arms wrapped themselves around her waist and pulled her to himself. The entire world could watch them at that moment, and she wouldn't have cared or noticed. She was with the man she loved, and he loved her back, and his kiss proved that to be true.

She looked up at him, smirking when he pulled back.

"Did I ever tell you how incredibly sexy you are in your dress blues?" she asked.

"I've been told that a time or two elsewhere, but never by you," he said, as she drowned in his hazel eyes.

"Let me tell you right now, you are."

"Let me tell you, I've never seen you looking more beautiful than you are right now. Even if your nose is a little pink still."

She grabbed his neck and kissed him again. She savored the way he kissed her, adored the way she fit perfectly against him, and ran her fingers through his soft hair. He was hers. All hers. And she would not let him walk away heartbroken this time.

After all the picture taking was done, everyone made their way to the reception center. Ted never looked so proud as when he walked his daughter down the short aisle. Tom and Alisa said their vows and exchanged rings. Then the party got started. Ted and Alisa got their dance, Tom and Alisa got theirs, and then a few other couples joined them on the dance floor. Caleb stood up and held his hand out to Paige. "Dance with me?"

"I'd love to."

He took her in his arms and whirled her around the dance floor until the music slowed down. He looked deep into her eyes. "I'll be flying home in a couple of days."

"I know."

"And I'm not sure when my CO will let me have more time off after all this."

"Then we'll have to make do with the time we have, and make the most of it."

"Said like a true military wife," he said, meaning swimming in his eyes. "I love you, Paige. I'd prefer not to be apart any longer than we have to be. We've already spent so much time apart. What I'm saying, Paige, is I want you to marry me. Will you marry me?"

Paige blinked her eyes so fast, trying to keep the tears from falling. She lay her head against Caleb's chest. "I can't wait to marry you, Caleb."

"Was that a yes?"

"Yes, it was."

He reached into his pocket and pulled out a ring. Paige gasped. He'd already gotten the ring. It was an emerald-cut diamond solitaire on a simple silver band. "It's a new one. And it can be a promise ring if you'd like something else."

"No, Caleb. It's perfect." He slipped her ring on her finger.

"Oh, no!" Paige said, looking up at Caleb.

"What?"

"What about my dad? My parents?"

"Don't worry. I spoke to your dad. The day we went to give Tom a blessing. In fact, he was the one who asked me what my intentions with you were."

"Oh, my gosh," Paige said, putting her forehead against his chest. "My dad."

"He was right. He knew. And he gave me permission before I even asked for it. And while I was at the temple with Tom, I asked our other Father too. He said it was an excellent idea."

Paige chuckled through her tears.

"I love you, Caleb Watson," she said. "I can't believe we finally get to do this life together. The Lord's timing doesn't always seem perfect, but seems everything worked out anyway. I'm so happy now."

"I love you, too, Paige Watson," Caleb said with a cheeky grin.

"Paige Watson. That sounds kind of awesome," Paige mused.

"I have to agree."

Chapter 31

The sun was scorching, but a slightly cooler breeze washed up on the shore every time a wave crashed against it. Paige was glad for the umbrella she lounged under nonetheless. Her pasty white skin was apt to burn then turn white again. She didn't even get the benefit of tanning. She found the beach peaceful for now. Caleb wasn't around.

Paige rubbed her belly absently as she turned the page of the book she'd been reading. She looked around the sandy area. It occurred to her she hadn't seen or heard Caleb for a while. She stood up on her beach towel and looked around. Foley Field Beach on Hilton Head wasn't really that crowded for this time of day. There wasn't any sign of him.

Suddenly, she felt herself swept off her feet from behind.

"Ha, ha, ha," Caleb cackled.

"Caleb, what are you doing?"

"You're suggesting I can't carry my wife around if I want to?"

"I guess you could, but—"

He started running for the shoreline.

"Caleb. No. Don't. You're such a jerk!" she screamed and laughed. As soon as he hit the bigger swells, he dumped her into the water. She jumped up, wringing the excess water out of her sopping hair. "Agh, my hair was almost dry."

She ran up to him and jumped on his back. "Back to my towel, soldier."

"Officer."

"Whatever. Marine."

He piggy-backed her back up the beach. Once they got back, he deposited her back down on her towel.

"Where did you run off to?" Paige said when he plopped down on the towel next to hers.

"I forgot my cell phone in the car," he said. "I checked to see if I was being called up with this next round."

"And?"

"Nope, we're good for a while."

Paige let her breath go. She leaned over and kissed him. "Well, even if you were, you know we'd be here waiting for you."

"I'd hope so," Caleb said, tucking some of her wet hair behind her ear. "Now that we're together, I'd like to spend as little time apart as possible."

"We'll make do. Every military family goes through it."

Paige leaned back on her towel, a wide grin on her face. She wiggled her toes letting her legs soak up the afternoon sun.

3 - 2 - 1, she thought.

"Wait. What did you mean by we? Alisa and Tom are at Pendleton right now. *You* would wait for me until I got home, if they called me up." He lay down on his towel again, but his face was deep in thought. "You said *we,* right?"

"Yes, I did."

"Military family . . ." he mumbled to himself. Suddenly, his head popped up off the towel. "Paige, are you—"

She kissed him again. "Yes, I am."

"You are?" he said, sitting up and wrapping her up in his arms. "We're having a baby? Our baby?"

"Yes."

"When did you find out?"

"This morning."

"Okay, we've been at the beach for most of today, and you're only just telling me now?"

"I wanted to see if they called you up first. I knew that they were getting ready to send guys out soon."

He leaned her back against the towel. He rubbed her tummy and kissed her softly. "I love you so much."

"And I love you. I'm so excited. We're going to be parents. You will be the best dad."

"We're going to be a family," he said. He gave her a remorseful look. "I'm sorry I threw you in the water."

Paige laughed. "I'm pregnant, not fragile."

"So, you're saying I can throw you in again?" he said, with her favorite wicked grin.

"No."

A Note from the Author

If you enjoyed reading Always Faithful, please consider leaving a review! It doesn't matter where, really—on Amazon, Goodreads, or your own social media. Reviews are like gold to an indie author and I appreciate them so very much!

Newsletter

Don't forget to sign up for my Book News newsletter! Get the latest book information, sneak peeks, and exclusive content for subscribers only!

ABOUT THE AUTHOR

WS Deming loves writing romance. Her passion is fueled by binge watching BBC's "Pride and Prejudice" and "North and South" at least once a year, watching cheesy romance movies, and her ability to quote almost every 80s teen movie. She lives in a little grey house in the West Desert of Utah, referees three kids, two cats and a dog. When she's not obsessively writing something she's going to the movies, crocheting things people won't wear, and talking geek with fellow geeks.

Check out my website!

www.ingramcontent.com/pod-product-compliance
Lightning Source LLC
LaVergne TN
LVHW050626100826
845148LV00011B/1746